Readers love *Planting His Dream*
by ANDREW GREY

"Andrew Grey gives us another good book about finding love and holding on to it despite tremendous odds."
—The Blogger Girls

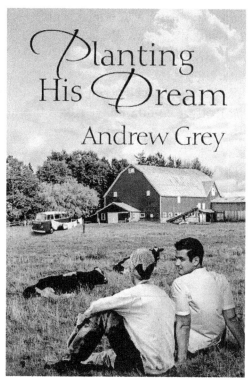

"Yet again Andrew Grey has managed to capture my imagination by presenting a deceptively simple situation in a light that made it interesting, revealing, and very moving. Bravo!"
—Rainbow Book Reviews

"This was a very well written book from an author I've grown to love."
—Inked Rainbow Reads

"I really enjoyed this story and it was very sweet."
—Scattered Thought and Rogue Words

More praise for
ANDREW GREY

Cleansing Flame

"For fans of the author—you'll love this—and for someone looking for a nice, sweet, hurt/comfort romance with a bonus, historical story—this is for you!"
—The Blogger Girls

"This was such a well-written story and the plot was woven together so perfectly, I couldn't have asked for more."
—Alpha Book Club

Poppy's Secret

"If you love a good second chance story, family, cute kids and an allover fabulous romance with a touch of hot man sex you will love this."
—TTC Books and More

"I really enjoyed reading this sweet story."
—Gay Book Reviews

Fire and Hail

"I absolutely LOVE this series and this newest addition is without a doubt a wonderful welcome."
—Diverse Reader

"Overall, this story was just another great addition to an already amazing series."
—Two Chicks Obsessed

Published by DREAMSPINNER PRESS
www.dreamspinnnerpress.com

Published by DREAMSPINNER PRESS
www.dreamspinnerpress.com

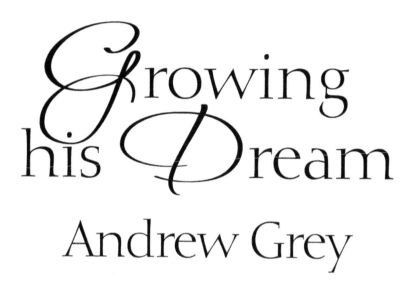

Growing his Dream

Andrew Grey

DREAMSPINNER PRESS

Published by
DREAMSPINNER PRESS

5032 Capital Circle SW, Suite 2, PMB# 279, Tallahassee, FL 32305-7886 USA
www.dreamspinnerpress.com

Growing His Dream
© 2017 Andrew Grey.

Cover Art
© 2017 L.C. Chase.
http://www.lcchase.com
Cover content is for illustrative purposes only and any person depicted on the cover is a model.

ISBN: 978-1-63533-812-6
Digital ISBN: 978-1-63533-813-3
Library of Congress Control Number: 2017905513
Published June 2017
v. 1.0

Printed in the United States of America

This paper meets the requirements of
ANSI/NISO Z39.48-1992 (Permanence of Paper).

To Dominic. He always made my dreams come true.

CHAPTER 1

LACHLAN BUTTAR'S feet hurt already. He'd been walking for an hour and was getting short of breath. His shoes pinched the side of his foot with each step unless he tilted it a little, but after a while, that made his ankle ache.

On either side of the road, empty fields with the stubs of last year's corn crop sticking out of the ground provided very little in the way of a view. Stopping at a country intersection, he looked ahead, as well as left and right, trying to figure out which way he should go. Not that it mattered very much.

His goal was to try to make it to Grand Rapids. Maybe there he could find work and try to figure out what he was going to do now. He knew the city was east, which was the way he was heading.

April could be a great time of year, but today wasn't one of those days. He crossed the intersection and kept going. Standing in one place wasn't going to get him any closer to his destination, despite how much his feet hurt. They didn't matter; nothing mattered. It wasn't like he had better shoes he could wear. These were the only ones he had, and they hadn't even been new when he'd gotten them. To take his mind off the pain as he trudged along, the asphalt stretching as far as he could see, Lachlan tried to think of better Aprils, something to raise his spirits and occupy his mind.

Two years earlier, in what seemed like a completely different era, his mother had taken him on a vacation. She'd won some sort of contest, at least that's what she'd told him. So she'd taken him out of school and they'd gotten on a plane and flown to Orlando, where they had spent four days in the parks. Somewhere in his backpack, he'd stuffed the dusky blue hat with Mickey on it that she'd bought him while they were there. He'd gotten to do everything imaginable while

1

on that trip and was the happiest he could remember being. Well, at least it was the last happy time he could remember. After they'd gotten home, she'd told him the truth. There was no contest and the trip had been a charade of sorts, a last happy interlude before she gave him the news that would change his life forever and ultimately lead to him walking down a country road with the clouds overhead getting lower and heavier. It wasn't going to be long before he'd need to haul out the small pink umbrella he'd stuffed in his pack. It had been his mother's, and he hadn't wanted to leave it behind.

Lachlan's steps grew more torturous as he continued, the pain he'd been trying to ignore becoming impossible. He sat on an old stump and breathed a sigh of relief as the sharp pain became a dull ache and slowly receded. He didn't dare take his right shoe off to rub his foot and make it feel better. It was likely swollen, and putting his shoe back on would be agony. Normally his feet were fine, but these shoes were… well, maybe he'd be better off barefoot. Lachlan got back up and continued on, one step at a time, and after a while, the secondhand shoes that were probably one size too small didn't hurt so much anymore.

Knowing he had miles left to go, he picked up his pace, since walking faster would mean he'd get where he needed to go all that much sooner. Of course, that was when the rain started. Not just a mist, but a spring rain, full-on. Lachlan got out the umbrella, opened it, and held the small amount of cover right over him, walking on. The umbrella did a good job of keeping his upper body dry, but his lower pant legs were soon wet and his shoes and socks soaked through.

The pain in his foot came back with a vengeance a few minutes later, and Lachlan looked around for some sort of shelter. There were a few buildings ahead, and he single-mindedly headed for them.

He approached a farmhouse that, with its peeling white paint, looked as aching and miserable in this rain as Lachlan felt, but he was becoming desperate and turned off the road to walk up the drive. He took three steps, and a dog—big, black, and barking up a storm—raced around the side of the house, coming right for him. Lachlan turned back around and walked as fast as he could to the road, thankful the dog stopped at the end of the driveway, barking its fool head off, snarling, and watching after him. So Lachlan trudged on.

He crossed another intersection, the moisture seeming to climb his body, seeping deeper under his clothes, sapping away the heat. Misery joined his pain, but he had no other choice—he had to keep going. On the corner he passed what looked like a small stand of some sort, and Lachlan wondered if it was unlocked. He tried the door but it didn't open. God, if he could only crawl inside, he'd have some shelter from the rain and would be able to rest for a while. No such luck.

At the next driveway, he stopped, wondering if there was another dog set to come at him. He didn't see one. All he saw were cows huddled together, black-and-white beasts under an overhang, waiting out the rain.

Lachlan walked up the drive, half dragging his aching foot, which caught on a rock. He lost his balance, tried to catch himself, and managed to, partway, and at least he didn't go head over heels. He ended up in the ditch, his feet and legs in frigid water. "Damn it," he swore as his misery increased even more. Lachlan got up and groaned. The umbrella, his only shelter, was bent and torn. He tried to fix it, but that only made things worse and the spines just broke off.

He wanted to cry, but instead closed it and threw it on the ground. He didn't know what to do.

"Young man!" someone called. "Did you hurt yourself?" An old lady under a large black umbrella was walking slowly toward him.

He took stock and realized he wasn't hurt, just cold. "Only wet, I guess."

She came close enough to look him over. "You better come inside with me. You'll catch your death out here. This isn't going to let up until tomorrow." She turned to peer up both sides of the road. "Did you walk from town?"

"Yes, ma'am." Lachlan looked down at his soaked shoes, wriggling his toes in an effort to try to warm them. It was futile, and he began to shiver.

"On a day like this? Are you touched in the head?" She ran her gaze over him, taking him in. "You don't seem crazy." She came closer still, her brown eyes meeting his. "You definitely don't have the look, and I should know. I've met plenty of crazy in my life."

Lachlan might have smiled if he wasn't wet and cold and his foot didn't throb. The thought of taking another step was too much to bear.

"Come on, honey. Let's get you inside." She motioned him ahead, and Lachlan put one foot in front of the other, trying not to wince with every step. "What did you do?"

"It's the shoes, I think—" Lachlan shut his mouth. No one needed to hear his sob story. He straightened, ignored the pain, and walked to where he'd first seen her. Lachlan held the door for her, and after she went inside, he followed. He stopped in the mudroom, dripping all over the floor and not wanting to go any farther.

"Katie, what's going on?" another woman asked. She was in a light blue blouse and jeans, with an apron on, her hair just turning gray, and Lachlan figured she was related somehow.

"I found me a drowned rat. This young'un walked from town. I'm not sure where he was headed, but as wet as he is, the logical place would be to the hospital with pneumonia if he doesn't get warm."

The other woman blinked at him. "Okay. I'll go get some of Foster's clothes so he can get dry, and you heat up some soup. He needs to be warm on the inside too."

"Where is Foster?"

"He and Abe are in the barn, getting ready for milking, I'm sure. Javi made a run into town. He wanted to pick up the tiller from the repair shop." She left the room, and Katie hung up her umbrella.

"Go ahead and get those shoes and socks off." She went into the nearby bathroom and handed him a towel. "Dry what you can. I'm going to start heating you up something hot." Smiling, she waved a hand in the direction the other woman had gone. "That was Harriet, my daughter-in-law. She'll bring you some dry clothes. I'm Katie. Just call me Grandma Katie, like everyone else."

"I'm Lachlan."

4

"Didn't I see you at church a few weeks ago?" Grandma Katie opened the refrigerator and hauled out a plastic bowl. She opened it, and the enticing scent of food reached his nose.

"Yes, ma'am, you might have. I was staying with the reverend for a little bit, and he brought me with him." Lachlan dried his face and hair as Harriet returned with a small bundle of clothes.

"Change into these and come back out. We'll get you fed, and you can tell us what you were doing walking all the way out here on a day like this."

"Thank you." Lachlan took the clothes and went into the bathroom. He closed the door and stripped off his wet things. Once he was in dry clothes, he instantly felt better, and the bone-deep weariness that had started to settle in caught up with him. His breathing was easier and his lungs no longer ached, though. That was a big improvement, even if his feet still hurt like hell. Clean, dry socks helped too. While he was in the bathroom, he washed his hands and face, feeling a little fresher.

Lachlan folded his wet clothes, and when he stepped out, Harriet took them. She turned and stopped, holding up a sock. "Are you bleeding?"

"It must be my shoes. I—"

Harriet hurried out of the room and returned a few seconds later. "Sit down and take off the socks." Lachlan complied, and she tutted and tsked as she looked over his feet.

"The good salve is in the cupboard upstairs," Grandma Katie told her.

"I'll get it. You stay there." She hurried out of the room, and Lachlan sat still, a little afraid to move. These two were like a whirlwind of care and concern, something he hadn't felt in a while, and he didn't want to do anything to upset the applecart. When Harriet returned, she treated his feet and helped him get the socks back on. "You need to rest for a while. Your feet are a mess. Where did you get these shoes?" Harriet went over and picked them up off the mudroom floor, examining them.

"The charity bin at the church," Lachlan admitted, feeling a blush creep over his skin.

Grandma Katie brought over a steaming bowl of soup and placed it in front of him, along with a huge glass of apple juice and a plate of bread. "Eat up, young man."

Lachlan didn't need to be told twice. He picked up the spoon and tucked into the beef noodle soup as if it were manna from heaven. Hell, maybe it was, and these two women were angels in disguise. "Thank you." He took a bite of bread, homemade, and damn near groaned. "This is really good."

"Slow down, hon. There's more, and no one is going to take it away from you." Grandma Katie sat in the chair across from him at the scarred farmhouse table. "How long has it been since you've eaten?"

"I guess a day."

Harriet placed a mug in front of Grandma Katie, then sat down herself. "Maybe you'd better tell us what happened."

Lachlan nodded as he took another bite of soup, the heat warming him as the heartiness filled his belly. "I don't know where to start."

"How old are you?" Grandma Katie asked. "Do we need to contact foster care or the state or something?"

"Seventeen. I'll be eighteen in, like, two weeks. They aren't going to do anything because as soon as I become an adult, I'll be too old for the system."

"Do you go to school?"

Lachlan shrugged. "I did, but not now I guess." Leaving had changed everything. He continued eating and slowed down after a few minutes as his stomach filled and the ravenous hunger that gnawed at him abated. "My mom and I lived in Ravenna. We moved there a few years ago. Things were good. She worked at the bank there…."

"What happened to her?"

He swallowed, his throat suddenly dry. "She died of cancer and there wasn't any money. We had a nice apartment above one of the stores, but I couldn't afford the rent and had to leave. I took what I could with me, but most of our stuff was just…." There was no use getting emotional over all this because there was nothing he could do about it. Everything was gone. Not that they'd had very much to begin with.

"What about your father?" Harriet asked.

Lachlan shrugged again. It had only been him and his mom for as far back as he could remember. He finished his soup and took a bite of bread.

"So is that why you were walking? Where were you trying to get to?"

"I had no place to go. I thought if I could get to the city…. Grand Rapids isn't that far away, and maybe I could get a job and earn enough money to live. But as you can see, I didn't think things out very well." He was about to continue his story when the back door opened and two guys, older than him, walked inside.

"What's going on?" the bigger of the two asked with an air of authority.

"Foster," Harriet said, "this is Lachlan…."

"Lachlan Buttar."

"He was walking to GR in this mess," Grandma Katie said in a tone that brooked no argument. "This is my grandson, Foster." She turned to the other guy. "Abe, he's our full-time hand." She got up from her chair as Lachlan greeted each of them with a smile. "You all done with the milking?"

"Yes," Foster grumbled. "Bob called. They lowered the price of milk again. It just gets up to the point where we can get ahead and goes right back down." Foster sat down and extended his hand. "It's good to meet you."

A third man came in, carrying bags that he placed on the counter. He came right over to hug Katie and Harriet before putting his arms around Foster's neck from behind. Noticing Lachlan, he smiled. "Hi. I'm Javi."

"He's Foster's partner," Grandma Katie explained.

Lachlan wondered if the term "partner" meant what he thought and hoped it did.

Javi sat next to Foster, with Abe next to Harriet. "What were you walking for?" Javi looked him over and then turned to Harriet. "Why is he in Foster's clothes?" Clearly Javi didn't miss anything.

7

Before Harriet could answer, Grandma Katie spoke. "He was soaked from the rain and ended up going ass over teakettle into the ravine. I wasn't going to let him freeze." No one argued with her. "I saw him in church a few weeks ago," she added for emphasis.

"I was staying with the reverend for a while." Lachlan saw Abe staring at him and he shifted nervously in his chair.

"I've seen you there too," Abe said gently, shaking his head.

Lachlan wanted to crawl under the table and die of embarrassment. If Abe had been in church, then he'd probably seen the most miserable, embarrassing, gut-punching day of Lachlan's life, and Lachlan wanted nothing more than to put that behind him. But his humiliation would live on.

Abe didn't look away, and Lachlan wished he had somewhere else to be. His stomach fluttered and his skin warmed under the watchful gaze of Abe's intense, sky-blue eyes.

"Here. Go ahead and eat." Grandma Katie placed bowls of soup in front of Foster and Abe. Then she took Lachlan's bowl and returned with one for Javi, as well as a second helping for him.

Lachlan thanked her. There was no way he was going to turn down an extra-big meal. Once he left, he had no idea how long it would be before he got a chance to eat again.

"How is the garden planning coming?" Foster asked Javi.

"Well, I think we have it drawn up and finished. Now that the tiller is fixed, I can turn up everything, and I thought we might add to the strawberry patch. I can till the adjacent area this year, and the plants will pretty much grow in on their own for next year. I'd like to do more, but we're running out of space."

"Unless we want to go into vegetables in an even bigger way, I think we're nearing our size limit." Foster ate his soup, and Lachlan did the same, listening but not saying anything. He shot quick glances at Abe, who looked back sometimes.

Gosh, Abe was…. It was hard for Lachlan to explain. He had a nice smile, even if there was a slight gap between his front teeth. His brownish-blond hair was long and hung a little in his eyes. He kept brushing the locks away, though they fell right back, but the

8

motion gave Lachlan a nice view of Abe's thick arms, especially where his shirt gripped the muscle. Lachlan tried to think of how he could describe Abe and decided on ruggedly handsome. As soon as the words entered his mind, he began to blush and turned away. He shouldn't be thinking of other guys that way. That had been made abundantly clear.

Lachlan finished his soup and looked out the window. The rain beat down, and the thought of going back out in that left him chilled to the bone, but he had no other choice. These people had been nice to him, given him a chance to get warm, and fed him. That was more than he had a right to expect from anyone. He sighed. "I should be going."

"Nonsense," Grandma Katie said as she turned to peer out the window. "It's still raining and way too cold." She turned to Foster. "He hurt his feet and they were bleeding when he took off his shoes."

"I don't want to be a burden to anyone," Lachlan said quietly.

Abe turned to Foster, biting his lower lip.

"We have more work than we can finish, and Foster, you were just saying that we needed to find some help for a week or two in order to make sure we're ready for planting." Javi looked Lachlan up and down. "Have you done farm work before?"

"Like milking cows?" Lachlan shook his head. "I've cut grass and weeded flower beds. I took care of both our neighbors' yards before my mom and I moved here. I can do just about anything." A seed of hope sprang to life inside him. "What sort of work do you need done?"

"There are some fences that need to be repaired, and I need someone to clean out the equipment sheds and clear out the vegetable stand by the street. Grandma Katie could use some help in the basement, reorganizing what's down there." Foster continued rattling off a list as Lachlan tried to keep it all straight. Then he turned to Javi, smiled, and swung back to him. "Are those things you think you can do?"

"Yes." At least he'd have a roof over his head and food to eat.

"Good. In exchange, we'll give you a place to stay and feed you. We start tomorrow. The rain is supposed to be over, and if it's sunny, the ground will dry out and we can finish the spring cleanup chores and get on to the preparations for planting." Foster pushed his empty bowl away. "I also want to clear that area between the barn and the equipment shed."

"You mean the graveyard?" Abe asked.

"Yeah. We need to get everything out of there. We'll strip what we can for parts, and then I'm going to call a hauling company to get rid of it all. It has some scrap value."

"What are you going to do there?" Harriet asked.

"I've been toying with the idea for a while. Grandma and Javi have been making cheese to sell at the markets, and we have a following. So I was thinking that we should build there and open our own creamery to make ice cream and cheeses and a few other artisan products from our own milk. If prices stay low, we can still make money by adding value to our products. For ice cream, I'd have to figure out a way to bring a freezer to the market, but we have time to work that out. We do have power."

"That's a lot of work," Harriet commented.

"Maybe." Javi took Foster's hand, and any sort of doubt about the kind of relationship they had was made instantly clear. For the first time in weeks, Lachlan relaxed. Foster and Javi were like him, and no one else seemed to care or get mad about it. "But we need another year-round business."

"Javi will be in charge of the creamery once it's built and up and running. I've been doing some research, and it's surprisingly easy to get started. We will need to build a separate building to house it, get proper equipment, and be inspected. But that's not a problem since the inspectors are the same ones we have already."

"How much will this cost?" Harriet asked.

"It will take about half our savings, but we've been putting that money aside so we could expand the farm. I had originally thought it would be more land and additional milking stock. But we can use some of it for this, as well as some additional acreage and milkers to support the creamery operation. The good thing is that we can grow over time. Start simple and see what happens from there. If it doesn't work out, we can use the additional space to develop the milking operation."

"You've given this some thought, then?" Harriet asked, not quite sold on the idea if Lachlan was reading her right.

"Clearly," Grandma Katie said. "We've all been working to get the operation on a sound footing for the last two years, and Foster has done that. Vegetables are only going to get us so far, and I think as long as we use only quality, natural ingredients, this creamery could be a real winner." She turned to Foster. "My mother used to make the most amazing peach ice cream. I remember how she did it. If you really want to do this, then Javi and I could work up some recipes that will knock their socks off. Ice creams the way they used to be, instead of all this fake stuff they put in them now."

"Let's talk about it some more a little later," Harriet said, and the others let the topic drop.

Lachlan's foot ached under the table, and he stood once the others were done but wasn't sure where he should go.

"Come with me," Grandma Katie said, leading him into the living room. She sat in the recliner and motioned Lachlan to the sofa while she turned on the television. "Go ahead and put your feet up. It isn't often we get a rest day here." She picked up some knitting beside the chair and went to work, her fingers moving and the needles clicking slightly.

Lachlan sat still, trying to remain as invisible and out of the way as possible. It had been made pretty apparent that he wasn't worth having around. After all, he was homeless, without a family, and seventeen. Basically, no use to anyone, as was clearly demonstrated last week at church. Lachlan appreciated what Grandma Katie and Harriet had done for him, and he intended to pay them back.

"Lachlan," Harriet said as she came in and sat beside him. "Try on these shoes and see if they fit. I bought them for Foster, but he says they're a little too small."

She handed him the tennis shoes, and Lachlan gingerly put them on. He sighed. They actually fit and felt good. His feet still hurt pretty badly, but when he stood, they didn't rub and hurt him further. "Thank you." Lachlan sat back down, but he felt strange not doing anything.

Foster stuck his head in the room. "Mom, I'm going out to the barn. Call me if you need anything."

"All right. Is Javi going with you?"

Foster nodded.

"Do you need help?" Lachlan asked.

"Well…."

"He's sitting right here, keeping me company," Grandma Katie said. She turned to Lachlan. "You need to stay off those feet. They were bleeding, and if they don't heal, they'll get infected."

"Grandma's right, as usual. Rest. There will be plenty of work to do tomorrow when it isn't raining cats and dogs." To his mom, he said, "When you get a chance, take Lachlan upstairs and show him the guest room."

"I'll take care of it," Grandma Katie said without stopping her knitting.

Foster left the room, and so did Harriet. Lachlan heard her working in the kitchen over the sound of the television. After a while, Grandma Katie's needles stilled and soft snores came from her chair. He sat back and closed his eyes, not meaning to doze off. But he was warm and full and had a place to stay for the night, and that was enough to lull him to sleep.

CHAPTER 2

FOSTER SAT at the kitchen table, a mug of coffee in front of him.

"The barn is closed, and everything is all set for tomorrow," Abe Armitage said as he joined Foster. The milking was done, the cows had shelter from the weather, and Abe was wiped out. Weather like this always took more energy than other days.

"Are you heading home?"

Abe nodded but didn't get up.

"Abe told me something you need to hear," Javi said softly as he came in.

"What's going on?" Harriet asked, coming into the kitchen, and Foster shrugged as she and Javi sat down.

"Well, I was in church last Sunday." Abe shook his head. "I don't usually go because they… well, they don't represent me, but my dad told me that I had to go and that he was tired of me missing services. I think he figures that they'll change me or something. Anyway, at the end of the service, Reverend Felder stood and said that there was a member of the community in need."

"We have plenty in need," Harriet said.

"This is different," Javi broke in, and she grew quiet.

"The reverend then brought Lachlan in front of the congregation and said that he'd been staying with his family for a few weeks and that he needed a home. He stood up there with an old ball cap in his hand, twisting it back and forth. It was so Dickensian."

"Like you know what that means," Foster teased.

"I read *A Christmas Carol* in school once—I know who Dickens was." Abe rolled his eyes. "The thing is, no one came forward. He just stood there, looking like he wanted to disappear, and it was obvious that the reverend, high and mighty as he is, just wanted Lachlan out of his house." Abe shuddered. He wasn't a fan of someone he saw as a hypocrite.

"And now he was walking out in the rain…."

"With no place to go." Harriet finished Foster's sentence for him. "He said he'll be eighteen soon."

"Yeah. I can't imagine trying to be on my own at his age without a home or anyone."

Abe could tell Foster's mind was already running a mile a minute by the intensity in his eyes.

"Mom, can you see about getting him back in school? He has to be close to graduating and he needs to do that. Lachlan can help here on the farm, and we'll give him an allowance and make sure he has what he needs."

That was why Abe thought the world of Foster. He always thought of other people and what they needed. Foster had given Abe a job on the farm a year ago, when he and his father hadn't been on speaking terms. They barely were now and at most tolerated each other. Abe didn't ask his father about his bible thumping, and his father didn't talk to Abe about the fact that he preferred boys to girls.

"I don't think I've ever seen anyone look so miserable as he did that Sunday." Abe kept trying to imagine how he'd feel if he'd been up there, and the only words that came to mind were *naked* and *completely exposed*.

"He said that his mother died of cancer not too long ago."

"Jesus," Abe breathed, stood, and went over to peek into the other room. Lachlan's eyes were closed and he looked so peaceful, without any of the worry and fear that had colored his expression only an hour earlier.

"Is he okay?" Harriet asked.

"Yes. He's asleep."

"He walked all the way here from the reverend's this morning with shoes that didn't fit and a jacket that hardly kept out the cold. He was looking to get away, and there was no one to stop him," Javi said. "I know how that feels. I walked a long way to get back here." Foster took Javi's hand, and a stab of jealousy went through Abe. Not

14

that he'd ever come between them, but Abe wanted what Foster and Javi had—each other and a family who supported and cared for them. "We'll help him."

"I know, sweetheart," Foster whispered, moving his head a little closer.

"I know what it feels like to be alone." The ache in Javi's tone was palpable, and Foster stood, taking Javi's hand, and led him out of the room.

Abe looked down at the tabletop as he heard them climb the stairs. "I should go home." He was the third wheel of a sort around here. Foster had given him a job and helped him out because his father wouldn't, though Abe wasn't interested in working for him anyway.

Harriet patted his hand. "I know things are difficult between you and your dad right now. He's a good man at heart. Rutland Armitage has helped us out a lot, and we've helped him. It's what we do here. Your dad is just confused about what he thinks is right. Foster and his father had the same sort of disagreements for a while."

"Yeah, but…."

She squeezed his hand. "You realize that a lot of this isn't about you being gay. It's about you growing up and coming into your own. Fathers always want their sons to follow in their footsteps, and they sometimes don't understand why their sons don't think the same way they do. Just give him a chance."

"Things are different now. Since Mom died last year, he's been a different man. Hard and stubborn all the time. He's thrown himself into the church, which isn't a bad thing, I suppose. It gives him a purpose besides always sitting at home in an empty house. But he listens to all that hellfire and brimstone junk and then he wants me to go along with him, but I can't. I won't. My dad wasn't an easy man growing up around. Mom was his heart and she tempered him, I think. Without that…."

"Give him time and be the person you are. That's all you can do."

Abe nodded and thanked her, pushing back the chair before standing. "I'll see you tomorrow morning."

She nodded and sipped her coffee.

Abe turned toward the back door and paused, then walked around the table to the living room. Lachlan was still asleep, his eyes fluttering, one leg shaking a little. He was the most beautiful, innocent person Abe had probably ever met, and just thinking about what he'd gone through broke his heart a little. After watching Lachlan's chest rise and fall for a few moments, he turned and stopped in the mudroom for his wet-weather gear before heading outside.

The rain had let up some. Abe climbed into the Escort sedan his dad had given him for graduation and drove the short distance home. At one time, his father's dairy operation had been as big as Foster's. But with his dad slowing down, the herd wasn't as large any longer.

Abe parked in his usual spot near the back door and got out.

"You done for the day?" his dad demanded as he closed the door to the milking barn, looking older than Abe could remember.

"Yes. You need help?"

"You think I'm too old to do my work?" his father challenged. "I'm done for the day, with no help from you." His father marched toward the house.

"I have a job."

"Tending someone else's herd." His father stopped and whipped around, water droplets flying off his head. "You spend your days working for someone else instead of here at home."

"Because of you. I like it there. They treat me right. And look at this place." He waved a hand. "You haven't done anything with it since Mom died, and I'm supposed to sit here and watch you let it fall to pieces? You aren't doing your job, so I'm going out to make a life for myself. Besides, you got Randy to help." He looked around. "Where is he anyway?" His older brother was everything his father could want: a perfect yes-man who didn't rock the boat and knew how to follow orders. "Why isn't he helping you?"

"He went to town, and I took care of the milking, and there's nothing wrong with the farm. It's the way it's been for a long time, and it works for us. The farm is fine. It's you I'm worried about."

"Dad...."

16

"Unchristian—"

"Stop!" Abe had had enough. Standing outside arguing with his dad wasn't going to do him any good. "This bible kick you're on is fine for you, but don't expect me to follow along."

His dad stalked over as the rain picked up, sluicing over both of them as they argued. "Your mother would be so disappointed if she knew."

Abe clenched his fists. "She did, Dad. I told her before she died. She didn't care. She held my hand and told me it was all right." Tears ran down his cheeks, washed invisible by the rain. "So whatever problems you have, they're all yours. Mom loved me no matter what." He walked toward the house to grab the back door. "That's a hell of a lot more than I can say for you."

He yanked the door open and stomped inside, took off his wet outer clothes, and went right on through to the kitchen. It pretty much looked as his mother had left it, except for the addition of a microwave, which his mother would never have had in her kitchen. His dad used it to heat up all the meals now. The sunny-yellow walls and dark wooden cabinets were exactly as they'd always been, along with the large table where they'd always eaten their meals as a family. Now they ate in front of the television most of the time. The house that used to be a home with his mother had become a place for him to sleep and little more.

His father thumped inside, footsteps heavy. "You eat?"

"Yes. I'm fine." Grandma Katie had fed him. She always did, bless her.

There were two chairs and a sofa in the living room. The one chair, battered and covered with a throw to hide the threadbare fabric, was his father's. The other had been his mother's and no one sat there. It was like a silent reminder that she was gone. The sofa was where Abe and Randy sat. Abe walked in, turned on the television, and tried his best to relax until his father came in with a plate in one hand and a beer in the other. He flopped down in his chair with two sandwiches stacked on his plate and changed the channel to whatever game was on.

Abe wasn't interested in basketball. His father watched whatever sports were on television. Long ago Abe had figured out that it didn't matter what his father watched as long as it wasn't what they'd been watching. Abe could have had the game on already, and when his father came in, he'd change the channel to something else just because he could.

He stood and left the room. If he argued, it would only start another fight, and they'd done enough of that lately. The best course of action was to leave.

He went up to his room and closed the scarred door. This entire house had seen two active boys, as well as whatever his dad and his sisters had done to the place. It was in need of more than a little care, maybe a complete renovation, but that wasn't going to happen. Not with his dad the way he was and money growing tighter. Abe closed the door and turned on the radio, then lay on his bed, the same one he'd had most of his life, looking up at the ceiling. Abe knew every crack and old stain in the plaster, but he barely noticed them. His attention wandered to Lachlan as he closed his eyes.

Abe's mind ran in circles. He couldn't seem to get past the mental picture of Lachlan asleep, almost angelic, on the sofa over at Foster's. Lachlan seemed so gentle and maybe even a touch broken. Not that Abe could blame him, after what he'd been through with his mother and then being put on display, his misery and loneliness front and center for everyone in the church to see.

His dad had actually leaned over to Randy and said that they could take him home, that Lachlan looked like someone who could work. As though he were a slave or something. The idea had made Abe's blood boil in the church, and just thinking about it now had his stomach roiling. His dad hadn't spoken up, thank goodness, and now Lachlan was at Foster's, where Harriet and Grandma Katie would take care of him, and maybe Lachlan would have a chance. He certainly had a better one than if his father had taken him in.

Abe lay still, his mind wandering but always returning to Lachlan. He'd only just seen the guy for the second time, but getting him out of his head was proving difficult. After a while, the room became stuffy, so Abe opened the window a little. Cool air rushed in, along with the sound of water dripping off the eaves. He was tired and figured he may as well go to bed. It wasn't that late, but years of farm work had taught him that the cows woke early and there was always work to do.

He got up and went into the bathroom to take a shower before returning to his room. He heard Randy and his father talking downstairs, but paid no attention to what they were saying. Instead, he got into bed. Tomorrow was going to be a busy day, and for some reason, he was looking forward to it. He knew he'd probably be working closely with a certain young blond for part of the day, and that was enough to put a smile on his face.

THE SUN wasn't up when he woke and got dressed. Abe shaved and cleaned up before quietly walking through the dark house and out to his car. There was no need to eat, because either Grandma Katie or Harriet would already be up and they'd have a real breakfast for him.

The lights were on in the barn at Foster's, and Abe went right inside.

"Just checking things over," Foster said before letting in the first cow.

He got into the swing of the milking process. He'd done this so many times, he didn't have to think about it any longer. "How's Lachlan?"

Foster paused, patting the cow's rump. "He woke at four in the morning, screaming. I don't know what it was about, and by the time I got there, he was asleep once again." He started attaching the milker to the next cow as Abe finished his. "Something happened to him at some point, but I'm not sure what. It could be him reliving the loss of his mother, but I don't see him screaming because of that."

Foster returned to work, and Abe did the same, his mind flowing to other things as his hands did what they'd done for most of his life. He could probably milk cows in his sleep, and hell, maybe he had a time or two. Getting up this early on a regular basis tended to promote a certain kind of mental filter where ingrained routine and muscle memory played a huge part in what he was doing.

"Did he say anything? I mean, did it sound like words he was saying?"

"No. It was fear," Foster muttered under his breath and then moved on. They changed the cows and got the new milkers ready while the beasts ate.

"Where's Javi this morning?"

"I let him sleep in. There's so much to try to get done today and tomorrow before it's supposed to rain again, and I figured the two of us could handle this."

Abe chuckled softly as he continued working.

"What?"

"Did you ever think you'd be this good a manager?" Abe finished up and stepped back, waiting for Foster.

"What are you talking about?" Foster asked, hands on his hips. "I'm a farmer."

"No, you're not. Well, you are, but that's not all you are. Think about it. You knew there was other work to do, so you let Javi sleep in so he wouldn't get too tired later. You also run every aspect of this place as efficiently as any farm I've seen. You think things out, develop new business opportunities like the creamery idea, and you thought about what might happen if it doesn't work out. That's a manager." He sighed. "Maybe if my dad had had some of those skills, there would be a place for me at home. But there isn't, unless I want to work as an indentured servant for the rest of my life." The farm was to go to his brother. His dad had already told him that. He didn't want it split up, so Randy was going to get it. "Dad figures that since we're his kids, we're free labor, and that's about the extent of his management skills. He isn't looking for anything new, so we're just hanging on."

Foster smiled slightly and shrugged, not taking his gaze off the cows. After a few seconds, he left, then returned with a shovel and wheelbarrow to clean up the cow plops. Abe got the hose and washed the floors. Once that batch of cows was done, they were turned out and the next group brought in, and the whole process started over again.

It was light when they finished, and thankfully the sky was clear, with streaks of red on wispy clouds set on a sea of blue. He and Foster trudged to the house, took off their boots and jackets in the mudroom, and joined Javi and Harriet in the kitchen.

"Where's Grandma Katie?" Foster asked. She was usually up by then. Sometimes Abe wondered how she did what she did at her age, but there was no stopping her, it seemed.

"She was up a couple times last night and was still tired, so I sent her back to bed for a while."

Harriet brought over a plate of eggs and ham, with toast and homemade jam on the table. Of course, there was a pitcher of milk on the table, and Abe poured a glass. He loved raw milk. For him it was the only way to drink it. Living on the farm, he'd had it all his life. "Thank you," he told Harriet.

"Sweetheart, you work hard, and feeding you is…." She placed a hand gently on his shoulder. "If you're going to work hard, you need something more than a sandwich for breakfast." She turned back to the stove.

"You know, there's a place next to the barn where we could build a coop and—"

"Nope. I hate chickens. Won't keep them or gather the eggs." Harriet glowered at both of them, and damned if Foster didn't snicker.

"Actually, I was going to suggest rabbits," Abe said. "If they're raised right, they can be delicious. The last time I was in Grand Rapids with Dad to sell the beef cattle he keeps on the side, the butcher said he was looking for someone to provide rabbit. Apparently there are a couple restaurants that have it on their menu and it's becoming popular." He took a bite of eggs and hummed. Harriet always put a touch of onion in them and, man, they tasted good.

"That's not a bad idea," Foster said between bites. "Let me look into it."

"You can't do everything," Harriet said.

Foster shook his head. "No. But with minimal investment, we can see if there's any way to make it worthwhile. I know how to clean and dress rabbits. We could start small and sell them at the farmer's market. There are lots of restaurants that shop there."

A shuffling sound from behind him made Abe turn as Lachlan came in, wearing the same clothes he'd had on yesterday. He was blinking, hair going every direction.

"I'll get you a plate, and Foster can go over what he wants you to do." Harriet returned, setting a full plate in front of Lachlan. "I washed your clothes, so you can wear them for today." She patted Lachlan's shoulder and then turned to Foster. "Later this afternoon I want to take him into town and get him some proper clothes and stuff."

"Good idea."

"Why would you do that?" Lachlan asked barely above a whisper.

"We all talked last night, and we need some more help, so you can stay here with us. You'll have chores to do, and on Monday you can go back to school," Harriet explained. "I'll take you in and we'll make sure you're all set to finish out the year. There's a bus that comes past, and we'll make sure they stop for you at the end of the drive. What about your books?"

"They are at the reverend's, I think." Lachlan stared at his plate.

"Then we'll stop there and get them."

Lachlan instantly stiffened and shook his head. "I never want to go back there."

"Okay. I'll stop and get them." Harriet sat down with her breakfast.

"I don't want to put you all out."

Abe opened his mouth to say that wasn't the case, but closed it again. It wasn't his place, even though he knew Foster and his family didn't think that way.

"You aren't," Javi said as he came in. Harriet made to get up, but he went to the stove and got his own plate, then took the place next to Foster. "You're welcome here." Javi turned to Foster, a pleading expression on his face.

Abe lowered his gaze to his plate to keep from smiling. He'd seen Javi use that look before, and Foster always gave in... every time. Usually those looks were for small things, but this time Abe got the feeling there was something deeper behind it, something only Foster and Javi knew. Instead of teasing and then telling Javi yes, Foster nodded, and an air of seriousness filled the room.

"Take Lachlan to town and make sure he has everything he needs. Do you have enough money? If not, take the debit card and get what you need."

"I can't let you do that. I have clothes... or I had clothes."

"What happened to them?" Abe asked.

"I couldn't pay the rent and got evicted. I didn't have a way of taking much with me, so a lot of stuff got left and...." Lachlan seemed on the verge of tears. "Most of my mom's things...."

"Do you still have the key?" Abe asked. When Lachlan nodded, Abe lifted his gaze to Foster and Javi. "Is it all right if I take him to town and we take a look?"

"Of course. Take the truck in case you need it." Foster set down his fork. "When did you get the notice?"

"A few weeks ago. The rent was due at the first of the month and I didn't have it, and I got the notices so I had to leave. I went to the church, and the reverend gave me a place to stay for a while, and...."

Abe clenched his fists. "And Reverend Felder never took you back to get your things or even check on the situation?"

Lachlan shook his head.

"Then finish your breakfast and we'll see what we can do." Abe dug in before looking up at Foster. "We'll be back as soon as we can." He finished eating, and Harriet brought in Lachlan's clothes. "Go ahead and change."

Lachlan ate his last bite, took his clothes, and left the room, thanking Harriet as he hurried out.

Abe finished his breakfast and took his plate as well as Lachlan's to the sink. Abe wasn't sure if there would be anything in Lachlan and his mother's place. He half expected to find that someone else had moved in, but it wasn't like there was pressure on the Ravenna rental market. Still, after the heartbreak in Lachlan's eyes when he spoke of what he'd left behind, Abe had to try.

When Lachlan came back down, Abe put on his regular shoes and ushered Lachlan out of the house and to the truck.

"Do you really think any of our stuff will still be there?" Lachlan sounded half broken.

"I don't know. All we can do is try. Just give me directions when we get closer and we'll do what we can." Abe started the truck and pulled out of the drive, heading to town. He knew there was a lot to do and time was limited, but he wanted to try to do this for Lachlan.

The small town of Ravenna was about six miles away, and at the center, he made the turn Lachlan indicated and pulled up in front of a rundown shop.

"We lived upstairs," Lachlan said.

"Okay. Stay here and I'll knock and see if the key still works." Abe got out, swung the door closed, and peered through the door on the side once he saw stairs going upward. Abe knocked and didn't get an answer, so he tried the key, and it turned the lock. Abe opened the door, and Lachlan got out of the truck, joined him, and then hurried up the stairs.

"It's our stuff," Lachlan called from the top of the stairs, bouncing on his heels. "It's still here."

The living room, tiny dining area, and kitchen were sparse, with little decoration and roller shades on the otherwise bare windows. Lachlan hurried to one of the closed doors and stepped inside. Abe followed. Like the rest of the house, the meager room held only a few touches that indicated a woman had occupied it.

"Get the things you want together, and I'll start taking them down to the truck. Start with the things of your mother's that you want to take."

"Okay," Lachlan answered blankly.

"Are there any suitcases?"

"Under the bed?"

Abe looked and found one. "Go ahead and pack this with what you want to take." He looked around. "What about the furniture?"

24

"It isn't ours. Mom and I moved a lot, so we didn't have much, and this place came furnished, such as it is."

"All right." Abe stepped back as Lachlan opened the drawers, searched them, and put some small things in the suitcase. "Can I help?"

"Sure. Wrap up the pictures on the dresser in some clothes and put them in the suitcase." Lachlan went through the other drawers and found a few small boxes that he added. With the suitcase full, Lachlan closed it and Abe took it out to the truck.

When he returned, there was another at the top of the stairs. Abe was about to take it down when he heard a muffled cry from the other room. He approached and opened the door. This had to be Lachlan's bedroom. It was as sparse as the rest of the house, with the exception of an old footlocker at the end of the bed.

"I don't…." Lachlan sat on the edge of the bed, rocking back and forth, holding a picture to his chest.

Abe sat down next to him. He hesitated at first, but pulled Lachlan into his arms, holding him. "It's okay."

"No, it won't be." Lachlan seemed to be trying to hold it together but wasn't able to for long. He buried his face against Abe's chest, his shoulders heaving as he managed to not make a sound while coming apart in Abe's arms.

"It will be okay. I can promise you that." He gently rubbed Lachlan's back, tears welling in his own eyes as the memory of losing his own mother became fresh once again.

Lachlan shook his head. "This is all that's left of her. An empty apartment that isn't even ours anymore and two suitcases. That's it." He sniffled and wiped his eyes, still clutching the picture to his chest. "She's gone. Just like that, she's dead and I'm alone." He didn't move from Abe's arms but stared down at his shoes. "It's not fair."

"No, it isn't. Things like this are never fair." Losing his own mother had been the most unfair thing that could possibly happen. "I lost my mom too. It really sucks, but I figured out a way to go on, and you will too. Sometimes it seems like the loss will never end. It never goes away completely, but it will fade." He wished he had better advice, but it was all he could think of.

"What am I going to do?" Lachlan began to shake, and Abe held him tighter, not knowing what else to do.

"First thing, you don't have to worry about a job and where you're going to live. Harriet and Foster meant what they said."

"How can they? None of you know me at all. I never met them before yesterday, and they're willing to give me a place to stay?" Lachlan pulled away. "There has to be a catch. There's always a catch when anyone does shit for you. They say they don't want anything… that they just want to help, but then they always want something in the end." Lachlan jumped to his feet and hurried to the closet. He pulled out a duffel bag and began stuffing clothes in it. "I don't even know why I'm doing any of this. I may as well just let it go because when I have to move on again, I can't take it with me." His arms flailed at lightning speed as he nearly ripped shirts off their hangers and jammed them into the bag.

Abe got up and gently placed his hand on Lachlan's arm to stop his frantic movement, then emptied the bag on the bed and began folding the clothes. "Harriet and Foster are the best people I know, and they mean what they say." He quickly folded the shirts the way his mother had taught him, then set them in a neat pile on the side of the bed.

"But why?"

"Javi's family used to work part of Foster's land. They came to pick asparagus a few years ago, and Javi and Foster got to know each other and fell in love. But Javi's family doesn't accept him, so he's on his own just as much as you are. Javi knows what you're going through."

"But his mother isn't dead," Lachlan said.

"No. But she may as well be. Foster loves Javi with everything he has and is, and he'd do anything for him."

"I don't get it." Lachlan sniffed once again and turned away.

"Foster knows how it feels to be alone because of Javi. It's been two years, and I think it still hurts Javi that his family doesn't have anything to do with him. Foster knows that and isn't going to turn you out. Neither is Harriet or Grandma Katie."

"But what do they want from me?" Lachlan asked, his voice touched with fear.

"Nothing. You'll have chores you need to do, but that's all." Abe narrowed his eyes. "Why? Did someone try to hurt you or something?"

Lachlan stiffened but didn't answer. Instead he went to his dresser, pulled open a drawer, and took out a couple pairs of worn tan pants and a few pairs of jeans. Abe folded them and added them to the small pile of clothing. He watched as Lachlan moved stiffly around the room, keeping his back to Abe if at all possible.

Fear welled inside Abe. Something was very wrong. Sure, Lachlan was hurting, but the way he was shutting out Abe was telling. He wasn't sure he was going to get anything out of Lachlan by questioning him, at least not at the moment, so he took the duffel bag lying in a heap on the bed and neatly put the folded clothes inside. "Is there more?"

Lachlan came around the side of the bed and opened the top drawer to add socks and underwear. "I guess not…." He scanned the room and sighed. "There isn't anything else here."

"What about the kitchen or other rooms?" Abe took the bag and set it next to the suitcase at the top of the stairs. "Is the television yours?" It looked ancient.

"No." Lachlan ambled into the kitchen and returned with a small box of things. "All our stuff fit in the trunk of my mom's car."

"Where is that right now?"

"It broke down just after Mom died and I didn't have the money to fix it, so it's sitting at the garage down the street. They said they'd put it out back for a while, but I don't know how long, and…." The abject misery was back, and Abe wished he knew what to do to try to help him.

"Do you know what's wrong with it?"

Lachlan shook his head.

Abe walked over to him and guided him to one of the tattered living room chairs. He sat down, and Abe got him a glass of water from the kitchen and handed it to him, sitting in the chair across from him. "Try to take things one step at a time. We'll get your things out of here so the landlord can't take them. Foster has plenty of room to store what you need him to."

"But why would he do that?"

"Because he's a good guy, and so is Javi." Abe took Lachlan's hand, not wanting him to feel alone, and as soon as he did, a little jolt of energy shot through him. Even miserable, Lachlan was beautiful, and Abe was willing to bet that with a smile on his face, Lachlan would be radiant. Abe was determined to somehow be the one to help him smile again. "What happened to you?" He gazed into Lachlan's big, sad eyes. The sad part didn't surprise him, but the fear he saw as well was nearly overwhelming.

Heavy footsteps on the stairs caught his attention. He released Lachlan's hands and turned toward the sound.

"Who's up there?" a deep, gruff voice barked.

"Mr. Hanson?" Lachlan asked, on the edge of tears once again.

"Yeah. Who are you?"

"Lachlan."

"I thought you were gone already." The footsteps continued, echoing through the space. "I was coming to clean things out. I have a new renter." Mr. Hanson entered the room, his hands on his hips. "You need to go now. This isn't your apartment anymore."

Abe jumped to his feet. "We know. He and I are getting his things, and we'll be gone in a few minutes."

"You have no right to be here. I should have changed the locks when I first kicked you out." He glared at Lachlan, and Abe saw red.

"I said we'd be gone in a little while. He's getting his clothes and personal things. Nothing more." Abe stood toe to toe with the bigger man. "You can give us a few minutes and we'll be out of here."

"How do I know you won't try to steal anything?"

Abe growled. "Like what? The television that's been around since the Stone Age? Give us a break. He just lost his mother, and all you can think about is how quickly you can rent the place?" He shook his head. "Just go and we'll be out of here soon." The man was a piece of shit and smelled worse than the barn after milking.

Mr. Hanson's gaze flicked over to Lachlan and then back to him. Abe had no intention of giving an inch. Lachlan needed someone to stand up for him and Abe would do it all day if he had to. "Fine. I'll give you an hour and then I'm coming in to clean the place out." He turned and stomped down the stairs.

"Are you okay?" Abe said. Lachlan was as white as a sheet.

"He looked like he might hit you."

"The guy's a blowhard. He likes to think he's a big, tough guy. But the strongest thing about him is his smell." Abe waved his hand in front of his face, and a ghost of a smile curled at the edge of Lachlan's lips. "Let's get anything else you want out of here before he comes back."

Lachlan nodded, got up, and slowly shuffled from room to room one more time. "I guess that's it."

"Then let's go." Abe grabbed the suitcase and duffel bag while Lachlan picked up the box, and they carried their load down the stairs and loaded it in the truck. Lachlan handed him the apartment keys, and Abe dropped them inside and locked the door.

"Is it stupid to feel like I'm leaving part of my mother behind? I know this was just an apartment and all, but it was our home, the last one we had before—" Lachlan got in the truck and pulled the door closed.

Abe got in as well. "No. When I first lost my mom, I used to go down to the kitchen in the middle of the night and just sit there because I wanted to be close to her. But you know your mom isn't there any more than mine was in the kitchen at home for me." He started the engine and pulled away. "She's in your heart. It took me a while to realize that. But my mom is always in mine, and yours will be too." He blinked to keep the threatening tears at bay. He hadn't expected to be this emotional, and maybe that's why Lachlan's words struck such a deep chord.

Abe wiped his eyes on his sleeve and drove back to the farm. He kept glancing at Lachlan and really noticed how young he was. Harriet was right. It didn't matter that Abe thought Lachlan was adorable and sexy as all hell. He needed to keep his distance. Abe

ANDREW GREY

could be Lachlan's friend, but that was it. It didn't matter that he wanted to be more. He'd protect Lachlan and help him as much as he could, but pursuing Lachlan was out of the question.

He pulled into the drive and parked the truck near the house, and Javi came right out to meet them.

"It looks like you had some success."

"Yes. Our stuff was still there," Lachlan said.

"Good. Go ahead and take it on up to your room." Javi smiled and helped Lachlan unload the truck. "I think Foster is in the barn," Javi told him, and Abe watched as Lachlan went inside, carrying his things. It wasn't until the door closed and he disappeared from view that Abe went to find Foster and get to work.

ABE THREW himself into his work, getting things done more quickly than usual. He wanted to make up for the time he'd taken in town, but he also needed to get his mind off Lachlan. Beautiful, attractive, and too-young Lachlan.

He finished his chores in the barn. Since Foster was checking on the herd, Abe started on the garden. The soil was damp from the rain, but firm enough to till, and they only had a few days before more rain was expected.

He was about halfway through the main vegetable bed, his arms vibrating from the shaking machine, when he noticed Lachlan walking out by the street, carrying a broom. The machine jumped, pulling Abe back to reality. He stopped the forward movement, watching Lachlan as he unlocked the fruit stand and went inside. Abe returned to his work, keeping an eye out in case Lachlan needed anything.

"I know you're watching him," Javi said over the hum of the motor.

Abe jumped and groaned under his breath. He'd been so absorbed in staring at where Lachlan was that he'd completely lost track of his surroundings and hadn't heard Javi approach.

"He needs someone to look out for him. But he doesn't need someone sexting him up." Javi flashed a smile, and Abe chuckled

30

at his incorrect usage of the term. Not that it mattered. Javi did that sometimes, but Abe understood what he meant.

"I'm not." The way Lachlan grabbed and held his attention was more than sex. Not that Abe was the most experienced guy in the world, but he wasn't a virgin... not completely anyway. "It's like he's been broken."

"He was. His mother died, left him alone. That's a lot for someone to take."

Abe shook his head. "I think there's more. Something else happened." He turned back toward the small stand as the door opened and Lachlan stepped out. Abe raised his hand in greeting, and Lachlan made his way over.

"I swept out everything and got rid of the mouse nest in the corner." Lachlan shivered a little—maybe it was the thought of mice, or maybe not. Abe wanted to know, but didn't want to push him. "I also swept off the shelves, and there were a few cobwebs, so I swept the ceiling too. So it's nice and clean. Maybe on a warmer day, we can hose everything down just to be sure."

"Good idea," Javi told him. "It will be a while before we can open it, but a spring cleaning was needed."

"What else do you want me to do?" Lachlan asked, so eager that he almost jumped out of his skin.

"Grandma Katie needs some help in the basement." Javi spoke gently, and a stab of jealousy surged through Abe as Lachlan responded to it by stepping closer to Javi.

Abe turned away and went back to work. He was not going to be jealous of Javi. That was the stupidest notion ever. Foster and Javi were solid, and Javi was one of the nicest guys Abe had ever met.

"Harriet said lunch is in an hour."

Abe raised his hand to acknowledge, determined to get the tilling done before then. He was just making a final pass when Harriet called him inside. He finished and put the tiller away, then headed inside, where he washed up and joined Foster at the table.

"I'm calling a halt for the day. It's Sunday, and we all need a rest. We were able to get most of what we needed done. I'll take care of the evening milking."

"I can help if you need it," Lachlan offered as he reached the top of the stairs behind Grandma Katie, who sat down and took deep breaths.

"Getting old really bites the big one." She sighed, and the others cracked up. "It's not funny—it's the truth. You'll all see soon enough."

"Did you get done what you needed to?"

"Yes," Grandma Katie answered as she scooted closer to the table. "I think I'm feeling a little under the weather, though."

Harriet brought a platter of beef roast, and Abe's stomach growled. Man, that smelled good, with mashed potatoes and home-canned vegetables. A real treat.

Lachlan sat next to him, and for a second, Abe forgot about his stomach as Lachlan's sweet scent overpowered everything else. He turned away and reminded himself once again that Lachlan was too young, no matter what his libido said.

"Go ahead and eat," Harriet told all of them, and Lachlan dug right in. Abe did as well, and Harriet joined them a few minutes later.

He loved meals like this. They reminded him of the ones his mother had cooked. He tried not to get too worked up, but his emotions were close to the surface after he'd helped Lachlan clean out the apartment. After lunch and helping Foster button up anything that he needed, Abe would head home and have to deal with his father for the rest of the day, and that was a prospect he wasn't looking forward to.

CHAPTER 3

"Happy birthday!" everyone shouted as Harriet brought a beautifully created homemade cake to the dining room table.

Lachlan could hardly believe they'd all gone to such trouble. There were even presents. He rubbed his eyes in what he hoped looked like disbelief, but really was a chance to clear the wetness that threatened to slide down his cheeks.

"Thank you, but this is too much." He smiled, and Harriet squeezed his shoulder.

"Blow out the candles and make a wish," Grandma Katie said as she took his hand. "Don't say what you wished for."

Lachlan didn't have to, because his real wish was already coming true. Foster, Harriet, and the entire family seemed to like having him around, and Lachlan had tried not to give them a reason to send him away. He worked hard and did every task he was asked to complete, giving everything he had. But he also lived in fear that if and when he messed up, they'd ask him to leave.

He made his wish and blew out all eighteen candles at once.

Abe came in the back door, arriving a little late. He added a present to the small pile and stood across the table. Lachlan's cheeks heated the way they always did when Abe was nearby, which hadn't been very often the last few days. Abe was usually busy, and so was Lachlan with homework and his chores.

"Open your presents," Javi said, with a huge smile on his face and his eyes filled with excitement as he handed Lachlan the first one.

"That's from Katie and me," Harriet said, and Lachlan unwrapped a new shirt and a pair of jeans, as well as a small box of chocolates. Lachlan adored chocolate and had mentioned it to Grandma Katie once, and she obviously remembered.

The next present was from Foster. It was a small box, and when he opened it, there was a set of keys.

"Javi and I got your mom's car from the garage and put new tires on it. So now you have something to drive." Foster grinned, and Lachlan's throat went completely dry. "We wanted you to have some freedom… and now you can take Grandma Katie into town when she needs to go to the doctor." He waggled his eyebrows, and Lachlan laughed. He'd take Grandma Katie anywhere—she was the grandmother he'd never had.

"Thank you. I don't—" Lachlan began, and Javi hugged him gently. Foster did the same, with more force. It was like something from a show on television, and Lachlan couldn't help wondering how long it would last.

"Here," Abe said, handing him the last package. "I made it myself."

Lachlan opened the box and pulled out a picture frame made of old, gray wood. Inside was a picture of him with Abe, Javi, and Foster. Harriet had taken it after they'd finished clearing the area Foster wanted to use for the creamery. They were all dusty, and Lachlan had a smudge on his smiling face. All of them together looked like a family. Lachlan swallowed and blinked away the threatening tears. He wasn't going to be sad today.

"Go ahead and cut the cake," Harriet told him, and Lachlan was hugely grateful for her interrupting his thoughts. She handed him the knife and removed the candles. Then Lachlan cut the chocolate cake and handed Abe the first piece. He cut one for everyone else, with the requested small piece for Grandma Katie, and finally one for himself.

"I didn't think I'd…." Lachlan hadn't thought he'd ever have a birthday celebration again. "Thank you all." He smiled.

"You're welcome, sweetheart," Harriet said, and they all ate their cake.

It was a Sunday afternoon and the sun shone brightly outside. They all lingered around the table, talking. Lachlan had come to love these Sunday afternoons when the farm seemed to slow down. It was a day off for all of them. Monday through Friday he went to school, then did his homework and his chores when he got back to the farm.

"Do you want me to start helping with the morning milking? I could do that before school," Lachlan asked Foster.

"No. I can handle that. I've done it all my life."

"Are you sure?" Harriet asked.

"Yes, Mom. Since I was twelve, I got up early, milked with Dad, and then went to school. I can't sleep in past five no matter how hard I try." Foster took Javi's hand. "Lachlan doesn't need to do that. It's more important that he get his sleep and do as well as he can in school." Foster turned to him. "Just keep doing what you're doing. You're helping us all out."

"Did you really start getting up that early at twelve?" Lachlan asked.

"Yeah. Dad needed the help." Foster sipped his coffee. "Dad couldn't afford to hire anyone. See, at the time the farm wasn't doing so well. We found out once Dad died that he'd been hiding debts. Anyway, I started helping with the milking, and it became time that Dad and I spent together. Granted, it wasn't fun by any means, but it was our time."

"So it's our bonding time now?" Abe smirked.

"Yeah, as long as you understand that I'm the daddy." Foster winked, and the two of them broke into peals of laughter. Lachlan and Javi chuckled, while Harriet and Grandma Katie seemed lost.

"You don't want to know," Javi assured them.

"When do we plant the garden?" Lachlan asked.

"You and Javi will do that starting in the next few weeks. It will take about a week for things to sprout, and we'll be beyond the threat of frost by then. It's supposed to rain on and off, so we'll work around that. In the meantime, the strawberry beds will need tending and any weeds pulled." Foster paused. "I also have a company coming in Wednesday to pour the foundations for the creamery addition. I decided to put up a pole building. It's cost-effective, relatively fast, and strong."

"But what if the creamery doesn't work out?" Harriet asked.

"Then we'll enlarge the connection to the barn and convert it to milking space. I planned it so no matter what, we'd be able to use the space. I stayed within the budget we agreed to."

"So you're going to need recipes?" Lachlan asked Grandma Katie. He really wanted to help.

"That's our department, boy," Grandma Katie told him. "I have some old recipes, and we'll start with those. Then we can test them out and make up some of our own." She patted his hand, and the excitement around the table ramped up all over again.

"I take it I'm the cheese part of the deal?" Javi said.

"That and general manager." Foster bumped Javi's shoulder. "Now that's enough business. This is a party." Foster grabbed his iPod, loaded it into the speaker, and raised the volume on "What a Wonderful World." Then he got up and took Javi's hand, leading him toward the living room, where he coaxed Javi into a dance. After a few minutes, Javi tugged Harriet to her feet, and Lachlan took Grandma Katie's hand, but she demurred.

Abe met his gaze and extended his hand. Lachlan swallowed hard and stood, then let Abe lead him to the living room. Just as they started, the music slowed, and Abe pulled him closer. Lachlan wasn't much of a dancer, but Abe's rich scent washed over him, and he tried to put some space between them as his errant body reacted.

"It's okay," Abe whispered into his ear. "Just relax and have some fun."

His cheeks heated, and Lachlan hid his face to keep from giving away his complete embarrassment at popping wood and having Abe feel it. Still, Abe guided him through the slow dance, rocking them back and forth. Eventually Lachlan rested his head on Abe's shoulder. The song ended and another came on. When Abe turned him, he realized that Harriet and Grandma Katie had left the room, leaving the boys to themselves. Javi clung to Foster, his arms around his neck as they danced.

"You feel nice," Abe said softly, holding Lachlan tighter.

It felt good to be held by someone again, and he put his head back down and just went where Abe wanted to go. It was his birthday and he felt special.

"Boys," Harriet interrupted as the song ended and the music grew faster. Lachlan stepped back and shook his head a little to clear the happy haze that had settled over him. "We have a problem." Her expression as serious as a headache, she said, "One of the fences must have come down because the cows are in the yard."

Foster raced to the kitchen and was already putting on his boots by the time Lachlan came in to do the same. "Abe, take Lachlan and find the fence break. Get it fixed while Javi and I find the cattle and get them herded back." Foster sighed, and as soon as his boots were on, Lachlan hurried and grabbed his jacket, heading out with the others. Javi ran to where Foster was already leading cows back toward the field.

"Let's go." Abe took off and Lachlan followed. They found the break in about five minutes. "I need to go get the truck and some wire. The posts are good but need to be reset. I'll bring back the digger and we can get started."

He hurried away, and Lachlan stayed there to keep any of the cows still in the field from getting out. A few ambled over, and he made noise to keep them away. They kept coming closer, so Lachlan waved his arms and yelled, and the cows finally moved away.

"What are you doing?"

"Keeping the cows from getting out," Lachlan answered as Abe handed him the post-hole digger.

"Have you ever used one?" Abe asked. Lachlan shook his head, so Abe demonstrated. "Foster is rounding up the cows pretty quickly. The dumb things want to get out, but they didn't go far. He's putting them in the other pasture, and once we get this fixed, he'll move them back in here."

"Okay." Lachlan got to work, getting the holes dug. Abe helped him get the posts set, and then they restrung the wire and attached it. By the time they were done, Foster and Javi had rounded up most of the cows. "Go ahead and help. I'll load the equipment." Lachlan began getting everything in the back of the truck, and Abe hurried away in the direction Foster had originally gone.

Lachlan got the post-hole digger and the tools in the back. As he hefted the new roll of surprisingly heavy barbed wire, he stepped in a patch of slick ground and his feet went out from under him. He tried to push the wire away, but it came down hard on his legs. He screamed as the barbs pierced his pants and skin in multiple places. "Abe...," he groaned, lying on his back, trying to breathe. Dampness crept under his clothes, every movement sending more pain racing through his legs.

He attempted to cry out for help but couldn't catch his breath. Lachlan closed his eyes and stayed as still as possible. His pants got wetter and he knew blood was seeping from his legs. He hoped he hadn't hit anything important, like a vein or something.

"Lachlan!"

"Javi," he managed to call, his lungs aching from where he'd had the wind knocked out of him.

"What happened?"

"I fell and the barbs went into my legs."

Javi lifted the coil, and Lachlan groaned, but at least the pain lessened and he was able to move. Javi took him under the arms and helped him across the yard and inside. "Harriet," Javi called, getting Lachlan in a chair.

"What happened?" Harriet asked as she hurried in.

"The roll of wire fell on his legs."

"We need to get your pants off." Harriet helped him up, and Lachlan opened his pants so Javi could help him get them off. His thighs and lower legs were peppered with scratches and punctures, with a few oozing deep red blood.

"What's going on?" Abe raced in, then skidded to a stop. "Oh, man."

"Get the alcohol." Harriet glanced up at Lachlan. "I know it will hurt, but I have to get this all cleaned so you don't get an infection. Do you know when you had a tetanus shot?"

"Last year," Lachlan groaned, just thinking about how the alcohol was going to burn.

Abe ran out of the room and pounded up the stairs. Harriet cleaned away the blood, and Abe arrived with the alcohol, handed it to her, then took Lachlan's hand. Harriet cleaned the wounds, and Lachlan closed his eyes, willing himself not to scream as waves of pain followed by cooling skin washed over him.

"I'll get him a blanket," Grandma Katie said, and Lachlan groaned as Harriet continued working. The entire family was now seeing him in his briefs. Talk about embarrassment on top of pain.

Instantly he was back in front of everyone at the church with a silent congregation, most of them trying not to look his way as the Reverend Jackass Felder went on and on about his plight in order to get rid of him. He shook his head, trying to get rid of the image, but it burned into his mind, replaying over and over.

Before he knew it, he was lifted off the chair. "Lachlan," Abe breathed. "Come back to me. It's over."

He turned his head to Abe's chest, burying his face as tears spilled out of his eyes.

"Your legs are going to be fine." Abe laid him on the sofa and spread a blanket over him. "Harriet bandaged the worst of the cuts."

"Thanks," Lachlan whispered, wondering how a nice birthday could turn so bad so quickly.

"I shouldn't have left you alone. That roll was heavy." Abe smoothed his hair out of his eyes, and Lachlan closed them again.

"Did you find all the cows?" Lachlan asked.

Abe sat on the edge of the sofa. "Foster is still looking for the last ones. Javi went back out to help."

Lachlan heard someone else approach, and he slid his eyes open.

Grandma Katie stood near the sofa with a glass of orange juice. "Drink this. It will make you feel better." She handed him the glass, and Lachlan sat up to drink the juice and handed the glass back. "You'll be okay. I had to throw out your jeans. The barbs ripped them up."

"Dang it." He didn't have that many clothes to begin with.

"I'll get you some of Foster's sweatpants. They'll be gentler on your legs while they heal." She settled him back down. "Just relax. You gave us all a scare."

"I didn't mean to." He closed his eyes again, mostly to block out his rising embarrassment. He'd freaked out in front of everyone. What were they going to think of him?

"It's all right." She sat in her chair and began knitting, needles flying in her practiced fingers. "What counts is that you're going to be all right." She paused after a few minutes and stood once again. "I forgot to get you some pants." She left the room, walking slowly.

"You did give us a scare. What happened?" Abe took his hand again. "I know it wasn't the pain. There was something else. You closed your eyes and swayed back and forth, and then you hummed something to yourself and started to shake. I'll help if I can."

"There's nothing you or anyone can do. I just have to deal with it and try to forget." He pulled the blanket up under his chin like a shield or a suit of armor in order to protect himself from Abe's sight, as though by looking at him, Abe would know what was going on inside. He couldn't have that. No one could know. Not that he'd be believed in the first place. "I'll be okay. It hurt but didn't cause much actual damage, and in a few days, I'll be right as rain." He needed to get back up so he could earn his keep. If he hadn't been so stupid and had watched his step, none of this would have happened.

"Okay." Abe patted his shoulder. "Just take it easy. I need to go out and make sure Foster doesn't need any help. But I'll be back to look in on you."

Lachlan nodded and waited for Abe to leave before closing his eyes once again. Grandma Katie returned and placed a pair of sweatpants over the arm of the sofa before taking her seat once more. She didn't say anything, which was a relief, and eventually Lachlan dozed off.

LACHLAN WOKE a while later, warm and a little confused. It took him a few minutes to remember where he was and that the unsettling dreams he'd had were just that—dreams. He wasn't back with the reverend and his family, but at the farm with Abe, Foster, and Javi. He was safe and it was his birthday. He got to make his own decisions now, and no one could lord it over him any longer.

Abe's voice drifted in from the other room. "I don't know. There's more to it than that."

"Did you ask him?" Harriet whispered.

"I tried, but he won't talk about it. Whatever it is, he thinks no one will believe him." Abe grew quiet, and Lachlan sat up. Grandma Katie's knitting rested beside her chair.

"Leave him alone. Sometimes men have to work through their own problems, and we don't need to be gossiping like hens while he's asleep." A chair scraped on the floor, and while the room was empty, Lachlan pulled on the sweatpants that had been brought down earlier. Then he went into the kitchen and sat gingerly in one of the chairs.

Harriet and Abe looked sheepish, which they should be, in his opinion, with the way they were talking. Lachlan hadn't heard anything bad, though, and it sort of proved they were genuinely concerned. But Grandma Katie was right. He needed to deal with this on his own. They couldn't do it for him.

"Where is everyone else?"

"Javi and Foster went into town. They decided to spend a little time alone and will probably see a movie or something before coming back." Harriet got up and brought him a mug of coffee. "Are your legs still hurting?"

"Yeah. Not as bad as they did, though." Lachlan figured in a day or two his legs were going to itch something terrible as the scrapes scabbed over and began to heal.

"I'll take a look at them tomorrow. I want to make sure there isn't any infection. Otherwise I'll call the doctor and have him take a look." She sat back down. "What did you and your mom usually do for your birthday?"

"Not a whole lot. Mom used to bake me a small cake and then she'd get me a present. It wasn't a huge thing." He sipped from the mug. Harriet usually made stiff coffee, but this was biting even for her. "I guess

I figured this one would be different or that I'd somehow feel different. I mean, I'm eighteen and an adult now."

"It's just a number, like a lot of ones you'll encounter as you get older. I remember when I turned forty, I thought I was over the hill, and then fifty wasn't too far behind that. And now, sixty is approaching."

"You're only as old as the one you feel," Grandma Katie said, then cackled.

Harriet tried to keep a straight face, and then she lost it too, and Lachlan followed. He'd heard the quip before, but coming from Grandma Katie, it was extra funny. He'd learned she was feisty, but sometimes she had almost comic timing and could deliver a line and then back away from it with skill.

"As I was saying," Harriet began again. "Don't put too much stock in a number just because it comes with a birthday attached. You've had to grow up faster than most people because of losing your mom." She sighed and circled her hands around her mug. "You'll graduate high school in a month."

"Yeah." He wasn't particularly excited about it. So much had changed recently, and now that he had little else in his life, he wished he had another year of school just for familiarity.

"What are you going to do afterward? Do you have any plans?" She sipped from her mug, and Lachlan understood what she was getting at. Harriet was asking how long he was planning to stay. Lachlan had been waiting for this to happen, and now that he was an adult, he was legally responsible for himself.

"Mom wanted me to go to college, and she helped me apply to some schools. But I can't afford it." He turned away. Just mentioning her caused his throat to close up. He wanted to crawl somewhere and cry his eyes out, but he wasn't going to do that now. He could fall to pieces once he was upstairs in his room and no one could see it.

Grandma Katie had been quiet for a while, but now she patted his arm and spoke up. "We aren't going to ask you to leave. That isn't what Harriet is saying." She took his hand and squeezed. "You need a family and you've got one here. We're just asking whether any plans have been made."

"Nothing yet." Everything had gotten away from him with his mother's passing. Lachlan hadn't had a chance to think about much of anything other than getting through the days with something to eat and clothes on his back.

"Did you get letters from the schools?" Abe asked.

"Yeah. They're in my things somewhere." His mind slid over the suitcases and boxes, unable or unwilling to latch onto them.

"Okay." Abe and Harriet shared a glance. "Can you find them?"

Lachlan nodded slowly.

"Then tomorrow we'll go over things, and we can figure out what your options are."

"But—"

Abe shook his head. "Lachlan. You need to make the most of the opportunities you have in life. I was never good in school. At home, working, that I was good at, but sitting still in class and listening to someone drone on about prime numbers or factorials was enough to put me to sleep. But I'll try to help you if I can."

"Okay." He breathed and slowly stood. "I'll find the letters tomorrow." Lachlan returned to the living room and sat down, staring blankly at the walls. This was all so much for him to deal with all at once. Everything happened at the same time—his mom, the apartment, graduating, college, and then…. He wanted to grab the blanket from the sofa and pull it over his head to hide from the entire world. He knew he couldn't do that, and it wouldn't do any good because the world would find him.

"Lachlan," Abe said as he sat next to him, gently putting his arm around his shoulders. "We just want to help you."

"I know. I'm some helpless, homeless kid that everyone needs to help." Anger and hurt melded together into a black ball that had to get out. Lachlan couldn't stop it, even if it was exactly how he felt.

"You're hurting, and you know it's okay."

Lachlan pulled away. "Are you going to offer to comfort me? I've had those offers before." He got to his feet, his legs aching with the sudden movement.

"What offers?" Abe asked, taking his hand but doing nothing more. "What are you saying? Did someone hurt you?"

The grip on Lachlan's hand tightened. He thought about yanking it away and leaving. He could go up to the room he was using and close the door, shut everyone out. Being alone had its advantages, but Abe's hand, his gentle touch, drew him here. He was almost afraid to move in case Abe pulled away.

"I'm fine." Lachlan's mind began withdrawing once more.

"You don't have to talk about it if you don't want to. I just want you to know that I'm here if you need me." Abe's voice broke, and Lachlan turned to look at him. He was surprised at the wetness in Abe's eyes. "I'm only trying to help."

"Why? I know you've been nice—everyone here has been really kind—but why? What did I do to make them want to be nice to me?"

"Not everyone is cruel or heartless," Abe said. "Foster and his family gave me a job when I needed one. I could have worked at my father's farm, but all I'd get there is recrimination and my dad thinking I was free labor for the rest of my life. Foster needed help and he offered me the job, and, though I didn't know it at the time, a place in their family. All farms aren't like this. Harriet and Katie, they help make this a home for everyone. Foster and Javi…." Abe smiled. "They fill this place with love. That's the best way to describe it. Just looking at them is enough to warm your heart."

"I still don't understand." But Lachlan found himself wanting to.

"I think it's pretty simple. This farm and the people on it are happy. They work hard and it isn't easy, but that doesn't matter. When you're happy, you want others to be happy." Abe paused and turned to him. "I don't know how else to explain it. The world out there can be pretty shitty. You know that. But not here. Foster and Javi help make things safe for us… people like us."

"You mean gay people?" Lachlan blushed a little.

"Yeah. My dad hates that I'm gay. He doesn't say anything about it because my brother, Randy, gave him hell the last time he said something."

"Your brother is okay with it?" Lachlan asked. So far all the people who had found out had decided that there was something wrong with him.

"Yeah. Randy isn't a bad guy. He wants to take over the farm. I used to want that too, until Dad said he wanted the farm to stay intact, so he was leaving all of it to Randy. Of course, that was after I told him I was gay." Abe huffed. "It doesn't matter because I need to figure out my own life."

"Did your mom know?"

"Yeah. I told her before she died. She understood and hugged me, telling me it didn't matter. I was still her baby. My dad didn't take it well. I thought it was because he was missing Mom and all of it got wrapped up together. But he hasn't changed and he might never. Did your mom know?"

Lachlan shook his head. He'd never told her, and now he wondered if he should have. Keeping secrets from her was something he hadn't liked doing, but she was the only family he had and he couldn't bear the thought of losing her. In the end he had lost her anyway and had never told her who he really was. "I never told anybody until…." He didn't want to talk about that… not now… not ever.

"It's all right."

"But don't people give you guys a hard time?" Lachlan half expected a mob with torches and pitchforks outside when he went to bed.

"Some people do. Most just mind their own business. Even my dad might say things, but he isn't going to do anything against Foster and Javi. He needs them. They have equipment that my dad uses. Most pieces of farm equipment are really expensive. Instead of everyone buying everything, they usually share and work together. It's the only way to make a go of it anymore, at least for small farms. Planters and harvesters are shared among multiple farms. My dad has a planter and Foster has a harvester. Everyone gets together and pretty much decides on a schedule to get everyone's fields done. So Dad keeps his mouth shut. Foster could afford to get his own planter if he needed to, but Dad can't afford any equipment right now."

Lachlan tried to follow the conversation. "So why is this farm so special?"

"Because Foster and Javi are prosperous and hardworking, and Foster isn't going to take any crap from anyone who gives him a hard time." Abe smiled. "There's also safety in numbers. Oh, and don't forget Grandma Katie. No one wants to cross her. Pissing her off isn't a good idea because everyone else likes and respects her."

"I can see that. I just don't know how to deal with it. I want to be like everyone else. Last year I tried dating… like all the other guys did, but she and I ended up as friends and now she's seeing someone else. I'm happy for her because if things had gotten serious, I wasn't sure what I was going to do." Lachlan took a deep breath to calm himself. "Lies build on top of lies, I know that."

"You don't have to lie here. Just be yourself." Abe turned as Lachlan did, and their gazes met, like a magnet pulling Lachlan closer. "Because the guy I see is pretty great. He's hardworking, kind, and caring."

Lachlan heard the words, but his attention centered on Abe's pink lips and how they moved. He licked his lips, wondering how Abe would taste. He'd been kissed before, mostly by Annabeth, the girl he dated for a while. The rest he kept pushed to the back of his mind. Abe drew closer, and Lachlan didn't move. He wasn't sure if he should move closer too. Instead, he stayed still, afraid Abe would change his mind.

Their lips met, and at first the touch was so gentle, Lachlan wasn't sure he was kissing Abe until he cracked his eyes open and Abe pressed a little closer. Abe tasted like fresh air and sunshine mixed with a hint of musk. Lachlan wanted more, and Abe held him tighter. Blood raced through Lachlan at lightning speed, draining from his head to parts lower that awakened with a vengeance. He pulled back, blinking and wondering if the kiss had been real or a dream.

"Was that okay?" Abe asked.

"It was nice." Lachlan smiled. He hadn't been expecting his first real guy kiss on his birthday. *Definitely a high point.* Lachlan told himself he wasn't going to worry about things. He had to finish school, and it looked like he had a place to stay for now. He and Abe would go over his college papers, and he could decide what was possible. And to top it all off, he'd been kissed by another guy. Abe… sexy and kind Abe, who made his heart race and caused him to actually wonder if what he'd been told and thought really was a crock of crap.

CHAPTER 4

THE NEXT two weeks were busy with preparations for the time when they were going to be really busy. Planting season was just around the corner, and there was equipment to check and repair, fields to prepare, and seeds to plant and set under lights in order to try to give them a head start. Abe was grateful that things with his dad had settled back into their usual quiet tolerance of each other, which meant that instead of fighting with his dad, Abe had more time to think about Lachlan, which he did every moment he wasn't occupied with anything else. Unfortunately Lachlan spent a lot of time out in the vegetable garden with Javi, so at the farm, Abe mostly saw Lachlan from afar and didn't get the chance to spend much time with him.

Abe knew that just because Lachlan was now eighteen didn't mean he was on the market. His instincts said to go slow. They'd kissed a few times and had had a chance to talk some, but mostly when Lachlan wasn't in school, they were either working or Lachlan was busy with homework or Abe was home.

"What's got you distracted?" Foster asked as they were finishing the milking. "As if I didn't know." When Abe didn't answer right away, Foster put his hands on his hips, lowering his head and glowering at him. "I have eyes and I see who you keep watching all the time. What's the problem?"

"Other than the fact that Lachlan is still in high school?" That was hard for him to get past, even if it was for just a few more weeks. Four years didn't sound like much, but it was a lot when Lachlan had just turned eighteen and Abe was on his way to twenty-three. "That and the fact that I don't get to see him?"

"You're working and he's in school. Did you expect that you'd end up seeing each other all the time? I don't see Javi all that much during work hours. He has his jobs and I have mine." Foster grabbed the hose and began cleaning the milking room floor.

"Okay. So, what do I do?"

"Besides sneaking off to clean the vegetable stand again and spending the time kissing and talking?"

Dang. He'd hoped Foster hadn't noticed.

"Try doing something nice. Like asking him on a date. Maybe think of someplace that he'd like to go and have some fun together."

Javi came in, and Foster set the hose aside to kiss his partner. "Yes, you should." He leaned against Foster. The two of them were so perfect for one another. Like they shared a brain and the skills that one of them lacked, the other had. "He needs to be treated as though he's special, though. So don't do anything cheesy."

Abe nodded. "I know he got hurt by someone, but he won't talk about it."

"Of course he won't. Lachlan has to learn to trust you and all of us. He isn't going to do that unless he can get to know you. So you need to ask him out like a gentleman and treat him like he's special." Javi entwined his arm with Foster's.

"I take it you did that for Javi?"

Javi nodded. "He did a lot. Some things I don't even think Foster realized at the time. So if you're interested in Lachlan, I suggest you lay off the kissing and use your lips for talking and getting to know him. He needs time, understanding, and gentle attention. Not being sexed up." Damn, Javi had a way of getting to the heart of things.

"Okay. Do you have any ideas?" Abe asked.

Foster opened his mouth, but Javi beat him to it.

"Do you expect us to do all the work for you? Think of something that comes from your heart. Not something that we suggest or something you think's expedient. That is, if you're serious about him." The intensity in Javi's eyes made him squirm.

Foster nodded slowly. "We have a little bit more to finish up here," he told Javi.

"I got it. You two go on," Abe volunteered. There wasn't that much left and he could handle it.

"You sure?"

"Yeah." Some time to think wasn't bad. "Go on and have some fun."

"Thanks, Abe," Javi said. "We'll return the favor when it's your date night." He winked and led Foster out of the barn. They reached the door and both chuckled softly, like they'd shared something only the two of them could possibly understand.

Abe finished cleaning the floor and checked the milk room to make sure everything was functioning properly. Then he turned out the lights, closed the doors, and headed out to his truck to drive home.

Lachlan must have been watching for him because he came out the back door to stand at the top of the steps as soon as Abe approached. "Hey." He smiled, his hands stuck deep in his pockets. "I've been real busy with school and stuff." Nervous energy poured off him.

"I know." Abe was just as nervous as he walked over. He wasn't sure if he should kiss Lachlan or not. Abe paused near the bottom step, half rocking from foot to foot. "I was wondering if you wanted to go out Friday night? I'm not sure what we'll do, but I thought it would be nice for us...." He should have practiced this in his head before he opened his mouth and sounded so completely inept.

"I think it would be nice to go to a movie or something." Lachlan looked inside. "Maybe Harriet or Grandma Katie would want to go."

Abe swallowed, his throat suddenly dry. "I wasn't thinking about that kind of evening out. I was asking you to come with me... on a date." He smiled, and Lachlan's lips formed an O and then he blushed scarlet. "Is that a yes?"

Lachlan giggled and covered his mouth with his hand, eyes widening in surprise. Abe wasn't sure if it was because of the date question or the fact that Lachlan had just giggled like a twelve-year-old girl. It hardly mattered when he lowered his hand to reveal a smile. A real smile. "Yes. I think that'd be nice. What do you want to do?"

"It's going to be a surprise." To him as well, because he had no idea yet. He wanted to come up with something Lachlan would like. Then he had it, just like that. "Wear comfortable clothes." He smiled as the idea took root and grew. This was going to be special. Abe hopped up the few steps between them and kissed Lachlan lightly on the cheek. "I need to get home, but I'll see you."

"Okay." Lachlan's voice broke, this time in a good way.

Abe headed back to his truck and got inside. He pulled down the drive, and his belly warmed as Lachlan stayed outside, watching him until he made the turn toward home.

When he arrived, Randy came out to meet him in the yard, appearing exhausted, with his dog, Pepper, right behind him. Even her tail seemed to be dragging.

"What's going on?" Abe asked as he closed the door to his truck.

Randy trudged closer, looking like his best friend had just died. "Dad took out a second mortgage a few years ago, and he's behind on some of the payments." Randy ran a hand through his hair and walked toward the house. "I used my half of the life insurance policy that Mom left for us to help bail him out. The bank manager agreed to meet with him tonight, and Dad's bringing the mortgage up-to-date, but I made him go over everything. We aren't making enough to get by."

Abe nodded. "I suspected as much."

Randy's eyes widened. "You knew?"

Abe motioned down the street. "That's what happened to Foster and Harriet a few years ago, and they diversified so they have something to fall back on instead of just dairy production. Why do you think they can afford to hire me?"

"You should be working here," Randy said without heat.

"No. This is going to be yours. Dad made that clear, so you need to take the reins and make some business decisions... move the farm forward. Dad is set in the past, and change is hard for him. And just so you know, I help plenty around here, even after working a full day, so don't pin this on me." His defenses rose. "You might try talking to Foster or even Javi instead of getting whiny at me."

Randy sighed and leaned down to pet Pepper. "You're right. If I want there to be a farm, then I need to step up." He looked around. "But where do I start?"

It was a daunting task. Abe knew some of the things that Foster had done and was working on, but those were things he'd learned sitting around the dinner table. They weren't to be shared, even with his own brother. "Like I said, talk to Foster. He's always full of ideas, and maybe there's something we can do in conjunction with him."

"Dad will never go for that. He doesn't say anything because we need Foster's equipment, but he isn't going to ask gay people for help. It would be admitting that they're smarter than him and better at business than he is."

"But they are. They did something rather than just let the farm go down the tubes. You can prop up and fix what Dad did with the mortgage, but if you're not making enough to cover expenses and run the farm, then you're... *we're* going to be right back where we started in six months or a year. Talk to Foster. We have space, and they have a stall at the farmer's market that draws a lot of customers. I won't tell Dad, and if nothing comes of it, then there's no harm done." Abe thought for a few minutes and then smiled.

"What did you just dream up?"

"Chickens," Abe said. "Harriet hates them. But we've raised them for eggs for years. So add some more and take the eggs to market. You could sell them and do pretty well. It's worth a try. Talk to Foster. I'm sure he'll help." He grew serious. "Look, if you want to keep the farm in the family, then maybe we have to do what we can in spite of Dad." Abe had always thought his brother needed to stand up to their father, but that was just his opinion. He and his dad fought because Abe was willing to stand up for what he believed and thought. "Do what you think is right for the farm."

"I will." Randy's expression brightened, and Pepper seemed to pick up on it, her tail wagging more vigorously.

"And talk to Foster."

"Yeah. I will." Randy walked toward the house, with Pepper right behind him. She went everywhere Randy did. When they'd first gotten Pepper, she was supposed to have been Abe's dog, but she'd bonded with Randy immediately. Abe had been upset at first, but that was years ago, and now those two were the best of friends.

Abe took a walk through the farm, looking at things with a critical eye. He could see where Dad had put things off and was maybe pushing some things off for too long. The milking area needed a fresh coat of paint, and some of the floor drain covers should be replaced. Little things that were done regularly at Foster's so they didn't become big jobs were going to be a real effort here. God, Randy was going to need help. There was no doubt about that.

After a little while, Abe went inside. Randy had a couple of frozen pizzas in the oven. Once they were done, he took a few slices and wolfed them down while watching some television. He kept expecting their dad to come home at any moment, but the house remained surprisingly quiet. Between the two of them, they finished off the pizzas and Abe went upstairs. Eventually he heard his father's truck in the driveway through his open window and soft whistling on the air. He didn't give his dad too much thought as his mind shifted back to Lachlan and the smile Abe had been able to put on his face.

"THE FOUNDATION looks good," Abe said on Friday as he approached where Foster was checking out the poured concrete floor and the vertical uprights for the pole building. All the concrete had to sit for a few weeks before work could continue, but it looked like Foster's creamery was starting to become a reality.

"You look nice. Are those new jeans?" Foster said with a grin as Javi came over.

"It's date night." Javi grinned and then turned to Foster. "Harriet and Grandma Katie are going out for dinner, so we'll have the house all to ourselves." He made this little circular motion with his hips that left Foster growling and Abe turning away. He didn't need that image in his head for the entire night.

"You're bad," Foster said with a soft chuckle. "Is Lachlan almost ready?"

"He's fussing upstairs." The door opened and snapped closed. "There he is."

Lachlan walked across the yard, with Abe watching every movement. He wore new jeans, blue and a little bit shiny yet, light gray shirt that caught the light, his intense eyes were filled with excitement, and his hair shone in the early evening light. "You said to dress comfortably, but I…." Lachlan lowered his gaze. "Is this okay?"

"It's perfect." Abe's throat was dry, and he had to wet his lips and swallow to get things moving again.

"Where are we going?" Lachlan asked excitedly.

"Head on out, you two," Foster said as he led Javi toward the house. "And have a good time."

Lachlan chuckled. "What are they in a hurry for?"

"Apparently they think they'll have the house to themselves tonight." Abe took Lachlan's hand and led him to the truck, then held the door open for him. He closed the door once Lachlan was inside, then hurried to the driver's side and got in. "I see you remembered the boots."

"You said to wear them." Lachlan pulled his feet close to the seat. "I didn't have any like these, so Harriet helped me get some from Goodwill."

"Don't be ashamed. I've had Goodwill clothes and shoes, boots—you name it." He started the engine. "Have you ever ridden a horse?" Abe asked.

"No." The excitement was back, and Lachlan buckled his seat belt. If he hadn't, he'd probably have hit his head on the roof, he was so excited. "Is that what we're going to do?"

"Yes. I went to school with Alexa Miller. She got married right out of high school, and she and her husband took over her dad's horse riding school and stable."

"So she'll teach me how to ride?" Lachlan asked as they headed down the road. "I never thought about horses." The delight in Lachlan's voice filled the cab of the truck, and Abe was pleased he'd chosen well.

"She'll take us out on a trail ride. The horse pretty much knows where to go, and you'll get to spend some time riding." He'd thought it would be fun and was thrilled that Lachlan had never been. "It's one of the beauties of living in the country. You can do things like that and it's not a big deal." Abe slowed down and turned left into the circular drive, then parked off to the side.

"Alexa," Abe called as she came out of the barn. He waved and waited for Lachlan before approaching.

"Abe! How have you been?" She hugged him and then turned to Lachlan. "I've seen you around town with your mom," she said and Lachlan nodded.

"She passed away a couple months ago," Abe told her.

"I'm sorry. Your mom always helped me at the bank. She was real nice." Alexa gave Lachlan a hug, and he held her.

Abe turned away. He knew talking about his mom was still hard for Lachlan, and if he needed a moment, Abe would give him his privacy.

When Lachlan pulled away, he rubbed his eyes.

"Lachlan has been staying with Foster and Javi for a few weeks now. And this is our first date." He knew she wouldn't have a problem with the two of them together. Alexa was a great gal, and she'd always carried a romance novel in high school. She'd even had a few gay ones, which was how they ended up as friends. Abe knew she'd understand.

"Foster and Javi are good people."

"He was staying with Felder before that," Abe said. Alexa threw him the weirdest look, and Abe wondered what it was that he didn't know about the good reverend. He'd never warmed to him, and his mom and grandmother never said anything bad about him, but they didn't praise him either, not like they had Reverend Neimi, his predecessor.

Alexa looked them both over. "You have boots, which is good. I've saddled up Gooseberry and Devil's Wind for the two of you."

"Devil's Wind?" Lachlan asked. "Sounds a little wild."

Alexa walked in step with Lachlan. "Actually, he's named that because he's the gassiest horse I have ever seen in my life. He's gentle, but you always want to be upwind."

"You're kidding," Lachlan said, smiling.

"Nope. Just wait. We'll put Abe on him and he can bring up the rear." She fanned herself, and Lachlan cackled like a loon. "You'll be on Gooseberry. Wait here, and I'll bring out the horses and help you get mounted."

She went inside and returned leading a chestnut-colored horse. Abe mounted easily and held Devil's Wind steady while Alexa led a deep brown mare around and talked Lachlan through mounting. "We'll only be half an hour or so. If we go longer, your legs will ache tomorrow."

"I feel like I'm going to fall off." Lachlan clutched the reins and held himself still in the saddle.

"Relax and grip him a little more with your legs. You aren't going to fall, and that feeling will pass in a few minutes. Just move with the horse and you won't get bounced around, and Gooseberry will be much happier." Alexa went into the barn once more, this time returning with a nearly black horse she said was named Matilda.

She headed off, and Lachlan fell in behind her, with Abe bringing up the rear. They were barely out of the yard when Devil's Wind demonstrated where his name came from. Abe held his breath as they kept going, waiting for the noxious air to clear.

"I told you," Alexa called from the front.

Lachlan laughed as Devil's Wind did a repeat as soon as the air cleared.

"Man." Abe patted his horse's neck. "Do you think you can lay off that stuff for a while? Huh?" Devil's Wind tossed his head. Thankfully he gave the gas a rest and Abe could concentrate on Lachlan, who had settled into the saddle remarkably well. His horse just followed Alexa's, but Lachlan moved well, rolling his hips so he didn't bounce. It was a beautiful sight, and from the hints of conversation, Lachlan was having a good time.

"Look," Lachlan called, pointing to the trees, which were breaking out their buds and leaves. "Spring is here and it's going to be beautiful."

"I love May. Everything comes alive!" The trees were blooming and trillium covered the forest floors, and for a few weeks, made it look like it had snowed again. Abe shifted his gaze from the flowers to Lachlan, and warmth spread through him when Lachlan turned to look at him, smiling gently. The light caught his hair, and for a second, a gold ring formed around his head. Yeah, Lachlan was an angel and he deserved his chance at wings, whatever that involved.

"It does." Lachlan turned back around, but everything about his posture screamed that he was having the time of his life.

They entered the trees, new greenery and flowers stretching overhead and underfoot. "There used to be an orchard on the property years ago, and some of these trees are the descendants. They grew from seeds. In the fall, we got all kinds of fruit. It's a real mixture, but gorgeous in the spring."

The breeze came up and white petals fell from the branches, swirling like snow in the air. It was magical. Lachlan tried to catch some of the blossoms, grinning when he glanced at Abe.

"Fun?"

"Yup," Lachlan called.

As the light lessened, they continued in a large loop, emerging from the trees and heading back across the fields toward the barn twenty minutes later. By the time they got back and Alexa helped Lachlan down, he bounced with even more excitement.

"You did really well," Alexa said to Lachlan as he rubbed Gooseberry's neck. Gooseberry nuzzled Lachlan's shirt, and he chuckled. "She's looking for a treat." Alexa handed Lachlan the reins, brought her horse into the barn, and returned with some carrots. "Hold your hand flat when you give it to her."

Lachlan held out his hand with the carrot, and Abe laughed when Gooseberry took it and Lachlan wiped his slobbered hand on his pants. "Thank you. That was awesome!"

"You're welcome. I'm glad you had a good time." Alexa led Gooseberry into the barn and then took Devil's Wind away, thankfully without a cloud of gas. She returned, and they said goodbye, with Abe passing her the price of the ride, plus a little extra, and then they headed to the truck.

"Back to the farm?" Lachlan asked, and Abe shook his head.

"That was just for starters. Come on. We'll have dinner, and then I thought we could go dancing. On Fridays the local roller rink puts away the skates and it's open for dancing. I thought it would be fun."

"But aren't people going to point and stare if we dance together?" Abe could feel Lachlan pulling away as he turned to look out the side window.

"You might be surprised." Abe continued driving, then entered the parking lot of a diner at the edge of town. "Have you been here?"

"No. Mom and I didn't have money to go out, so we ate at home, and I packed my lunches for school. So I don't know the restaurants at all other than to drive past."

"Then you're in for a treat. It doesn't look like much, but the chef worked in Grand Rapids and Ann Arbor before moving back here." Abe parked and got out, then waited for Lachlan before leading him inside. He was glad he'd called ahead for a table, because as usual the place was packed. Good food and great service brought people from all over.

"I have your table," Renae said from behind her desk. She led them through to a table by the side windows that overlooked the pond in the field next door. Lights shone over the water, and deer moved around the edge.

"Oh wow," Lachlan breathed as he stared out the window. Abe opened his menu to glance over it until Lachlan turned back. "Is it always like this?"

"Most of the time." Six deer clustered around the pond, drinking and eating before wandering away. "It's part of the fun in coming here. The deer provide a view for the restaurant, and in return for not allowing hunting, the restaurant gets their beef from right over there." Abe pointed to a distant barn behind the field. "They both win, and you'll never get a more amazing steak than right here."

"Cool." Lachlan glanced at the menu. "Just order what you know is good." He turned to continue looking out the window. "Before moving here, we always lived in town, so I didn't get to experience things like this up close... or ride horses." His eyes shone in the low light, reflecting his excitement.

When the server returned, Abe ordered, with Lachlan filling in how he wanted his steak and what he wanted on his potato.

"We have béarnaise sauce," the server offered, and Abe added it to both orders, explaining the tarragon butter sauce to Lachlan once she'd left.

"It's amazing."

Lachlan looked around. "But... this is a diner?"

"They have the usual diner staples, but with some extras too. When Marcello took over, the diner had been run by his mother for decades. He wanted to do something different, so he expanded the menu, and people responded to the new dishes. It's an odd mix, but it works, and people love that there's a place to get finer food in a town like this."

The server brought their drinks and salads, then quickly left them alone.

"So, what do we do on this date?" Lachlan asked. "I haven't been on very many, and mostly they were nervous affairs where we talked and hoped we didn't say anything completely stupid." He sipped his Coke as Abe chuckled.

"Let me see. I know you moved here about two years ago," Abe prompted.

"Yeah. Before that we lived outside Milwaukee. Mom had a head for numbers and worked in banks for as long as I could remember. She was the assistant branch manager in a small bank there, and when they took over the bank here, Mom was offered a job. They phrased it as a promotion and gave her a little more money. We moved here, and it turned out she was doing the same job she was there, just with a different title. She was supposed to be the branch manager and held that title, but there was a branch president who she reported to. It was all a bunch of title shifting. She always thought we'd made the move for nothing, but then she got sick and it didn't matter so much." Lachlan grew quiet for a few seconds and then snapped out of it. "Have you always lived here?"

"Yeah. I grew up on the farm, as did my dad. It's always been in the family. When my brother takes over, he'll be the fourth generation to run it."

"Do you feel bad that it won't be you?" Lachlan asked.

Abe shrugged. "I did. I mean, I know it's in part because my dad doesn't understand me being gay. He can be so stubborn sometimes. But if the farm is going to survive, it can't be split up, so one of us has to get it. And I want to make my own way." He drank some of his coffee and set the cup back down. "I used to dream about going to the city and making it big. I wanted to run a huge company and be this massive success. Of course, I had no idea how to make that happen." He smiled. "People who are really successful have a vision, like Foster does. I don't have that vision. I just wanted the success part." He shook his head, frowning a little. "I did okay in school, but not great, and didn't have much of a future. When Foster said he needed help, I was happy to take the job. At least I'd get paid for doing what I was doing at home for free because Dad thinks getting paid for work you do at home is sacrilege." Though what had been really going on was that Dad relied on free labor to continue running the farm.

"Mom always paid me an allowance for doing things to help her at home. It wasn't much because we didn't have a lot, and I had to get my own clothes. She bought stuff for my lunches for school, so I didn't have to pay for those." Lachlan stabbed at his salad and took a bite.

"Did you ever know your dad?"

"No. It was just Mom and me. She said he was a guy she knew from high school. Apparently she met him about ten years after school and they got involved. She got pregnant by accident. I guess the condom broke or something. As soon as he found out, he asked her to marry him, but then got cold feet and skipped town. Mom went home, and my grandmother helped her through the birth. But Mom and Grandma had a difference of opinion. Grandma said that Mom should give me up to my grandmother and let her raise me. Mom wasn't going to let that happen, and they didn't talk after that for quite a while. I think I get some of my stubbornness from her. Grandma died of cancer, the same as Mom, five years ago." Lachlan finished his salad, set his fork down, and stared at his empty plate. "I don't mean to be such a downer."

"You aren't." It hit Abe just how hard Lachlan's life had been. "Did you ever see your dad?"

Lachlan glanced up. "Once. A man came up to me in the grocery store when I was five and told me that I was his son. I remember looking at him, a total stranger, and telling him that I didn't have a dad. Then I hurried to find Mom. They had a fight, and I never saw him again. After that Mom got jobs with the bank and we ended up moving every few years."

"Do you think your mom was trying to keep you away from your dad?" Abe asked.

"I don't know. She didn't seem nervous or like she was looking over her shoulder. But it could have been a possibility. After over ten years, though, I don't think there's anything to it. Mom was always thinking that the pot of gold was just over the next hill, you know? She never stopped searching for it." Lachlan finished his Coke and played with the straw. "What was your mom like?"

Abe smiled. "She was super cool. She died a couple years ago in an accident. Dad has never recovered from the loss." The truth was that Abe missed her every day as well. "It was so sudden. I told her about being gay when she was in the hospital. She hung on for a while, but there was so much internal damage that they couldn't save her." Abe took a deep breath and slowly released it. "You know, we should talk about something else."

"Good idea," Lachlan agreed. "What do you like to do when you're not working?"

"Ride motorcycles. I have one in the shed at my dad's. I need to work on it and get it running, but I haven't had the time lately. How about you?"

"Maybe we could work on it together?" Lachlan offered.

"You know about motorcycles?" Abe was shocked. That was about the last thing he expected.

"I love engines and I used to want to be an engineer. That's what I was hoping to study in college. But it doesn't look like I'm going to be able to afford it. I got accepted to a number of schools. But how am I supposed to get the money together to go?"

"Where do you want to go?"

"I'd like to be able to go to the University of Michigan, but that isn't feasible, even with in-state discounts."

"There are loans and things. Do you have all the paperwork?" Abe asked.

"Yeah."

"Maybe you could ask Harriet to look things over and help you. I bet she'd be good at things like that. It's probably getting a little late."

"I checked the dates on the acceptance letters and I have to decide in the next week, but I don't think it matters much." Lachlan sighed, a heavy sound.

"It does. You're smart, and I've seen the hours you put into your homework. You can do whatever you want and go places I can only dream of. Don't sell yourself short. I'll help you if I can. We can sit down with Harriet tomorrow and figure out what your options are. Okay?"

Lachlan nodded.

"And yeah, I'd like to work on the motorcycle together. I got it when I was in high school and rode it everywhere. But it stopped running and I had to put it aside because I didn't have time for it any longer."

"What kind is it?" Lachlan asked.

"A 2006 Harley Sportster. I saved up for a year to buy it, and Mom chipped in to help me. It's a sweet ride."

"What's wrong with it?"

Abe shook his head. "I don't know. It might not be much. We'll get it out and can take a look at it." With working at the farm and then spending some hours helping his dad and brother on his days off, he hadn't had a lot of time for it, and it would be nice to have someone to work on it with.

"Awesome!" Lachlan's happy smile lit the room.

The server brought their steaks, and they looked amazing.

"Wow, this looks great." Lachlan inhaled deeply and groaned before digging in, dipping his first bite into the rich, creamy sauce. His groan sent heat racing through Abe, causing him to drop his fork, and it clattered on his plate. He snatched it back up and concentrated on his food rather than Lachlan's lips and jaw.

"Abeforce."

Abe winced as his real name drifted across the restaurant.

Lachlan held back a snicker.

"It's a family name. I hate it and never use it. Everyone thinks it's Abraham and I'm just fine with that."

"Who's that?" Lachlan whispered with a leftover smile from the name revelation.

"Marcello," Abe said as he approached their table. "Lachlan, this is Marcello."

"The chef." Lachlan shook his hand. "This is wonderful."

"I'm not a chef. Just a really good cook who feels that diner food should be more than burgers, french fries, and hot dogs." He smiled the way he always did. "I'm glad you're enjoying your meal."

"We are. Thank you," Lachlan said, seeming a little lost.

"I saw that you'd called ahead." Marcello glanced at Lachlan and then back to Abe. "Is this a special night?" His leer morphed into a smile. "It is, isn't it?"

"Yes. Lachlan and I are on a date." Abe smiled as Marcello kept looking at Lachlan. Marcello wasn't a poaching kind of guy, but the lust Abe saw when he turned back was enough for Abe to want to claw his eyes out, or at the very least, give him a fat lip.

"Then you have a wonderful evening. I just wanted to say hello." Marcello smiled again and walked back through the restaurant and into the kitchen.

"He seemed nice."

Abe glanced at Lachlan, considering. How did he want to explain about Marcello? "He's a good guy. When he first came back to the area, he and I saw each other a few times. It wasn't a

63

big deal, and we figured out we were better off as friends than as anything more."

Lachlan leaned over the table. "So, he's… gay?" He whispered the last word.

"Yeah. There are a few other couples around. Some keep a low profile, while others are out and proud. This is the country, and some people don't take to anyone who's different. But most people go about their business."

"I never knew." Lachlan sat back and returned to his meal. "So what else should we talk about?"

"Well," Abe said. "I was wondering, what do you have coming up in the last few weeks of school? I know graduation is in a month."

"Yeah. Mom had already ordered my cap and gown for me. I suppose I should go to the ceremony."

"What about prom?" Abe ate a bite of his steak, the sauce tangy and amazing.

"It's in a week. I wasn't going to go. I don't have a date, and it costs money to rent a tuxedo and all the things that go with it. Besides, I wasn't going to ask a girl to go with me, and I don't think I have the courage to go with another guy. I don't think the school is ready for that." Lachlan chuckled softly. "I imagine some of the guys in my class would shit bricks if they saw that, though."

"In general, do you like school?"

"Yeah. It's okay. All my teachers have been pretty understanding with what happened, and the counselor has made a point of checking that I'm doing all right." Lachlan seemed comfortable, and that was nice to see. "It's hard sometimes."

"I know. I still miss my mom. It sneaks up on me sometimes." He couldn't believe it. Every time they started talking about anything else, somehow they ended up talking about their mothers again. He'd been hoping to direct the conversation to something more cheerful. Although he needed to remember that for Lachlan, the loss was still so fresh. It had to be something he thought about almost constantly.

"I know. I thought I could be strong enough to handle whatever was coming and then…."

"Hey. It's okay to grieve." His dad was the stiff upper lip, never let anyone see you break down kind of guy, and the loss of Abe's mother was eating him alive. He was angry with the world and at life itself. Abe had tried to help and only gotten more anger thrown at him for his trouble. "I had to, and I probably still am." Movement caught his eye, and Abe turned and pointed. "Look out there."

"Awww." A mother and her fawn had come to drink. The little one was so cute. It moved carefully around the water, the mother standing guard as it drank. Lachlan was spellbound, his mouth hanging open a little as he watched, tongue licking his lips every few seconds. Abe needed to concentrate on something else and keep his mind from going down the naughty paths it kept trying to take. "They're so cute."

"Yeah, they are. There's a farm a few miles away that raises venison for restaurants. They have a couple dozen deer in high pens. I could take you over and you could see them up close if you wanted."

"Do you know everyone?"

"Pretty much. The area isn't that big, so between school, church, and the various parties and festivals, as well as the market, you get to know everyone. It's how small-town living works." He returned to his dinner, finishing off his steak and potato.

By the time they were done, they were both stuffed and declined dessert. Abe paid the bill and thanked their server before getting up. Marcello met them as they left and shook hands with both of them.

"You're an amazing cook," Lachlan told him. "You should open a restaurant."

"You're funny," Marcello quipped with a smile. "Thanks for coming."

Abe guided him out to the truck and drove to the other end of town. The roller rink parking lot was full, since it was the young people's Friday night hangout. He parked, and they got out.

"I'm nervous," Lachlan said, running a hand through his hair.

Abe smiled. "Don't be. Most people are here to talk, socialize, and have a good time, so relax and don't worry." He guided Lachlan toward the door, paid for their tickets, and they went inside.

The actual walls of the rink had been pushed back. The smooth wood floor shined, and strobe lights hung from the ceiling, flashing to the techno pulse. Already feeling uplifted, Abe moved to the beat as he found an empty table along the outer wall.

"Do you want anything to drink?" There was a bar of sorts that served soft drinks and snacks, but no alcohol. There were plenty of other places in town that served drinks.

"Bring whatever you're having." Lachlan sat, and as Abe turned away, he noticed Lachlan tapping his feet.

Abe smiled as he weaved around groups of people until he reached the snack bar area. He ordered two Cokes and took them back to the table, where Lachlan hunched away from a familiar figure.

"Hey, Eddie," Abe said as he approached and handed Lachlan his Coke. "How's it going? You know Lachlan… of course you do—he stayed with you for a few weeks."

"Yeah, Lachlan and I are good friends." Eddie leered at Lachlan, and Abe went on full alert. He'd never particularly liked Eddie Felder. In school he was always as sanctimonious as his father.

Lachlan had grown pale and his hand shook as he set his cup on the table. "The Felders were nice enough to give me a place to stay for a while." The ice in Lachlan's voice was unmistakable. "Thanks for coming over, Eddie. It looks like people are getting ready to dance, so you might want to find your date."

Eddie leaned closer to Lachlan. "Don't think I won't know where to find you if I need to."

"What are you doing?" Abe asked, grabbing Eddie's shoulder. "Leave him alone."

Eddie pulled himself to his full height, doing his best to puff himself up. "You just stay out of this."

"No. Go away before I break your nose again. Remember in eleventh grade? I put that bump in your nose, and this time I'll hit you hard enough, there won't be anything they can do with the ugly thing." Abe balled his fists, but Eddie growled and backed away, walking across the floor as though he owned the place. "Asshole."

"Of course you'd know him," Lachlan said in a small voice.

"Yeah. Eddie's just a bully. He thinks because his dad is the reverend that he has cover or something. His father thinks he's some kind of angel and refuses to believe anything else. He's as dumb as a box of rocks and likes to throw his weight around." Abe sat down. "He decided he was going to get under my skin in school years ago, and I cleaned his clock then and I'll do it again now." He kept an eye on the dark-haired lummox. Eddie always looked like he needed to shave and maybe have someone separate his eyebrows. Even though his father didn't believe in such things, Abe always thought Eddie was proof of the theory of evolution because the kid definitely looked like an ape.

"He came over to say hello," Lachlan said and grabbed his soda, sipping through his straw.

"That's not what it sounded like." Abe leaned a little closer.

"It was fine." Lachlan turned his gaze out toward the dance floor. His jaw dropped a little and he pointed to a couple in their late twenties or early thirties. "Wait… are they dancing together? I didn't expect that."

Abe grinned at him.

Lachlan looked back at him, smirking. "You knew, didn't you? That's what you were being cagey about earlier."

"Yup. Can you dance?" Abe loved how Lachlan smiled as he stared at the couple. He continued watching Peter and Rory as they moved together on the floor. They were terrific dancers, and watching them was definitely like seeing sex standing up. Peter had a way of rolling his hips that was most definitely seductive, and Rory played the part of his quarry to perfection, making it hard to pull his eyes away. Not that he wanted to come between them, but because the love and attraction between the two men was so enticing.

"Mom used to love to dance, and she made me her partner lots of times. We only danced in the living room. I'm not sure how good I'll be out there, next to them." Lachlan seemed to pull back his excitement. "People are going to be watching me."

"No more than they'll be watching anyone else." Abe continued watching, sipping his soda. Out of the corner of his vision, he saw someone moving toward Peter and Rory. Eddie, of course, his mouth set, eyes burning as he made his way forward.

"There's going to be trouble," Lachlan said, but Abe was already moving across the floor.

"Your kind isn't welcome here," Eddie was saying to Peter and Rory as Abe approached.

"No," he interrupted. "You're the one who isn't welcome." Abe had already clenched his fists in case Eddie got physical. "You need to leave or we'll have you removed." He flicked his gaze to the men at the door, and both security guys were already on their way over. They went right to Eddie, who had a reputation as a troublemaker.

"What's the trouble?"

"You let fags in here?" Eddie spat, straightening to seem more threatening.

"They weren't bothering anyone, but you are." The huge bouncer crossed his arms over his ample chest. "I think you've done enough and it's time for you to leave." He pointed toward the door. "Now!"

Eddie once again puffed himself up, but it wasn't going to work, so he turned in a huff, heading to the door.

"Thank you," Peter said to the bouncer.

"You're welcome." He followed Eddie while the second bouncer trailed behind.

"Now that's a breath of fresh air," Peter said with a smile. "He always carries a stench along with him."

Rory slipped an arm around Peter's waist. "Who's your friend?"

"Come on over," Abe invited, and they walked to where Lachlan was still sitting, watching them. Abe smiled and made introductions. "This is Lachlan. He moved here a few years ago."

"Is this a date?" Peter asked.

"A first date, yes," Lachlan answered, and Abe rested his hand on Lachlan's shoulder.

"It's so nice to meet you." Peter and Rory shook hands with Lachlan. "He and I moved out here a few years ago from Chicago," Peter explained, and Lachlan shifted around to the back of the table, allowing Peter and Rory to sit down. "We both had high-powered careers."

"I was in finance, and Peter was working toward a partnership in a law firm. Neither of us was happy, and we used to come to Saugatuck for vacation. One year we decided to explore and looked all around the area. We found our small farm as we were knocking about and fell in love with the place."

"What do you raise?" Lachlan asked.

"Heirloom vegetables and goats. Peter milks the goats and we make cheese that was picked up by Meijer's for their high-end deli. We're adding more goats so we can produce some more cheese, but then we'll be at peak capacity. We'll see where we can go from there. Neither of us is interested in growing to the point where we can't keep the quality perfect. We bought the farm so we could work with our hands and do what we really wanted while staying close to the land." Rory squeezed Peter's hand. "He and I both made a lot of money very young, but the pressure and demands became more than either of us wanted."

"We want to start a family." Peter smiled from ear to ear.

"Are you going to use a surrogate?" Lachlan asked.

Rory shook his head. "We're in touch with child services in the county, and we have decided to adopt two or three children who need a home." The way they looked at each other, overflowing with love, was strikingly beautiful, and it reminded Abe of the way Foster and Javi gazed at each other. It also made him want to be looked at that same way, like he was the center of everything. "Apparently there's a little girl who needs a home, and we're supposed to meet her on Monday."

"That's what we were celebrating this evening." Peter stood. "Let's go dance." His hips were already moving with the music.

Abe stood as well, and Lachlan allowed him to lead him to the floor. They formed a small group, which seemed to make Lachlan more comfortable. After a few minutes, he let loose, flowing his hips and arms to the music. Abe drew closer, putting his arms around Lachlan, who came right into his embrace.

If anyone looked at them funny or made comments, Abe didn't see or hear. His attention was on Lachlan, holding him. Lachlan lifted his face, their gazes met, and Abe was transported. Everyone else on the dance floor fell away. He only had eyes for Lachlan.

Abe licked his lips, and Lachlan did the same. He leaned closer, and Lachlan tilted his head slightly, agreeing silently to what Abe had been asking. It would be so easy to fall for Lachlan; he knew that. Just being around him made the world seem less bleak and was enough to brighten the grayest rainy day, but being the center of his attention was summer sunshine. Abe reveled in that warmth as they continued dancing.

Once the song ended, the music picked up tempo once again. Lachlan moved with the music, getting the hang of the dance, probably by watching Peter and Rory. Those two seemed to be the life of the party, and others gathered around them, creating a circle of writhing bodies. The energy was intoxicating, and Lachlan seemed just as caught up in it as Abe.

Song after song played, and hours passed in the blink of an eye. Abe got more drinks, and they both sucked them down.

"I don't feel so well," Lachlan said as Abe held him. "My head is spinning."

Rory and Peter stopped dancing and helped Abe get Lachlan seated at the table. "He looks a little out of it," Rory said gently. "Did you set your soda down?"

"Just for a minute," Lachlan answered.

Abe stood on his chair, looking out over the dance floor. He got the attention of one of the bouncers, then continued watching. Sure enough, he caught sight of Eddie on the far side of the room. The bastard smiled and then turned away, heading toward the door.

"What happened?" the bouncer asked.

"I think he was slipped a Mickey," Peter explained. "I'm not sure what it was."

"I saw Eddie in the club. He must have gotten back in. He was heading for the door. I know that asshole did this."

"Can you get him some water?" Peter asked Rory. "We need to get Lachlan out of here and into some fresh air."

"What is wrong with that guy?" Abe asked, not expecting an answer. The next time he saw Eddie, he was going to wring the bastard's neck, pastor's kid or not.

Abe helped Lachlan to his feet, then guided him through the club and outside into the air. Lachlan was becoming lethargic, and Peter was already on the phone with emergency services.

"An ambulance would be twenty minutes away. Take him to the RediMed center toward town. They should be able to help him, and it will be faster than getting him to the hospital."

"Thanks, guys," Abe said, lifting Lachlan into his arms. Lachlan leaned against him, and Abe wished it were under better circumstances. He put Lachlan into his truck and drove toward town. He pulled into the RediMed center with Lachlan groggy and semiresponsive. He got him out and carried him inside.

The attendant behind the counter took one look at him and ushered him right into the back room, asking questions as they went. "What happened?"

"We were dancing and I think someone slipped something into his soda. I'm not sure what, but he said his head was spinning and he's gotten sleepier."

"Okay. Put him in here." She opened a door, and Abe gently set Lachlan on the examining table. He wished he'd have thought to grab Lachlan's glass so it could be checked, though he wasn't sure if they did that sort of thing.

A doctor hurried in. "I'm Dr. Patterson. Can you tell me anything about what he might have taken?"

"I think he was given one of those date drugs."

"That would make him agreeable to anything." He checked Lachlan's eyes, shining a light in them. "Son, can you hear me?"

"Yeah," Lachlan giggled, squeezing his eyes closed. "You sound funny. Are you under water?" He lay still, and the doctor took his pulse and blood pressure as well.

"We got him to drink some water before we brought him here." Abe shoved his hands in his pockets, getting more worried by the second.

71

"We'll get him some more water and let him rest awhile. Usually these drugs work their way out of the system fairly quickly. He's still responsive, so he wasn't given too high a dose."

"I spilled my drink. Can I have another?" Lachlan slurred.

"We're getting you something," Abe told him.

The doctor sat back on his stool. "If he didn't drink it all, then he's lucky and should come around soon. Usually people snap out of it all at once. We'll keep him here until we know he's going to be okay."

"Thank you."

"Look, if you know who's doing this, the authorities need to know. We've had a rash of people being drugged lately, and most of them didn't have someone around to take care of them the way your friend had you." The doctor's dark expression left no doubt that he'd seen some pretty bad situations.

"I don't know who it was for sure. But I have a pretty good idea." And Abe intended to get to the bottom of this somehow.

The doctor didn't seem to want to let the issue go, but what Abe had told him was the truth. He didn't know for sure. "I'll have the nurse bring in some water for you." Then he left the room.

Abe stood next to Lachlan, holding his hand, his stomach doing loops and cartwheels. God, he hoped he didn't get sick while he waited.

"Are we still at the club?" Lachlan asked.

"No. We're at the doctor's," Abe told him as gently as his nervousness would allow. "Just relax. They're going to bring you some water and you need to drink it all."

"Okay." Lachlan smiled. When the nurse came in with a cup and pitcher, Abe poured a glass and Lachlan drank it without hesitation. Abe wondered if Lachlan would have drunk motor oil if that's what he'd been given. The absolute trust was endearing, but frightening at the same time. He could see the danger of this damn drug, and he wanted to kill Eddie.

Lachlan lay still, and Abe kept hoping he'd get better. He called Harriet and Foster to let them know where they were and what had happened. After half an hour, Lachlan opened his eyes and sat up, looking around. "Why am I here?" His voice was clear and he blinked a few times. "How come we aren't at the dance place?"

"You don't remember anything?" Abe asked, still holding Lachlan's hand.

The nurse came in. "You look much better." She smiled and took his pulse and blood pressure. "His vitals are much closer to normal, which is good. I'm going to let the doctor know. Also, you have some people out front waiting for you."

"I do?" Lachlan asked.

"I'll send them back." She left, and a few seconds later, Foster, Javi, Harriet, and Grandma Katie all came into the room, fussing over Lachlan and asking what happened.

Abe explained what they thought happened and who he believed had done it.

"Why?" Harriet asked, turning to Lachlan, who shrugged and lay back down.

"That boy was always trouble, and though the reverend is quick to see the issues with his congregation and to try to make sure they stay on the straight and narrow, he never was good at seeing what was right in front of him," Grandma Katie said as she held Lachlan's other hand. "I intend to have a talk with the man after services this Sunday about managing things closer to home."

"Please don't," Lachlan whispered. He closed his eyes. "My head hurts," he added with a sigh as the doctor crowded into the room.

"It looks like you have plenty of support," Dr. Patterson said to Lachlan. "Is this your family?"

Lachlan didn't answer right away, so Grandma Katie turned to the doctor. "You better believe it. Now what happened to him and is he going to be all right?"

"He's likely to have a headache for a while, and it's best if you take him home and get him to bed, but I believe he's going to be fine. Whoever slipped something into his drink didn't do him any favors."

Dr. Patterson handed Lachlan some papers, and they all got ready to leave. Foster stayed behind, and as Harriet and Grandma Katie ushered Lachlan outside, Abe saw Foster at the window, handing the woman a credit card.

Abe's heart ached. They had only known Lachlan for a few weeks and he was considered family. There was no hesitation about taking care of him. Somehow Abe doubted his own father would do much for him if he were in this situation other than maybe make sure he got a ride home.

When he got outside, the others were clustered around his truck.

"Sweetheart…," Harriet was saying in a rather plaintive tone.

"I really appreciate you all coming, but Abe can bring me home. We were on a date, and this—"

"Harriet, there's no need to mother hen. He'll be home a little while after us. Just don't be too long. You heard what the doctor said. You need to rest." God bless Grandma Katie. She made it clear Lachlan was going to get what he needed whether he wanted it or not.

Foster came out, and the four of them climbed into Harriet's car.

Lachlan got into the truck as Abe went around to the driver's side. "I'm sorry about all this," Lachlan said once Abe pulled out of the parking lot.

"Why? It's not your fault. Eddie Felder is a complete ass."

"Do you really think it was him?" Lachlan asked. "They escorted him out. How could that be?"

"I saw him in the club again. He must have gotten back in, and he saw me, challenged me. I know he put something in your drink. It wouldn't have taken long."

"Then it must have been him," Lachlan said, sighing. "He's done that stuff before." He stared at the floor, and Abe pulled the truck to the side of the road.

"He drugged you before?"

Lachlan sighed. "I don't think so. But he had a date with this girl, I don't know her name, and he brought her back to the house while I was staying there. His dad was out visiting parishioners. I don't think he was supposed to bring girls home, but he does what he wants. Anyway, I was up in the room they had given me to use, doing my homework, and I heard giggles from downstairs. I got thirsty and came down to get some water. By then the room was quiet, no giggles and stuff. I walked by and went to the kitchen. He had to have heard the water running, but it mustn't have mattered to him. On my way back, I was curious, so I went down to the family room and saw Eddie, bare-assed, on top of this girl, and she looked out of it."

"What did you do?" Abe gripped the wheel hard.

Lachlan looked out the window as he spoke. "I screamed and ran at him, pushing him off. The girl was groggy, and I did what I could to help her. I half expected Eddie to hit me, but I think he was afraid I'd tell his dad. Anyway, I helped get her dressed, and that's when Reverend Felder came in. Eddie tried to say that I'd brought the girl home and that this was all my fault. I protested loudly, but I don't think he believed me. It was easier to blame me than to think your kid could date-rape someone. That next Sunday was the day he dragged me in front of the congregation. He had to get rid of me somehow, and after that I knew I had to get the hell out of there."

"Jesus. Was the girl okay?"

"Yeah, but I don't know who she is. I hadn't seen her before." Lachlan put his hands over his face. "I know I should have done more to help, but I was scared to death, and Eddie made it clear that he'd see to it I was blamed. And who'd believe me over the reverend? I know the jackass would blame me to keep his precious kid from getting into trouble."

Abe put the truck in Park and slid over to hold Lachlan tightly. "Okay." God, even like this he smelled amazing. "There wasn't a lot you could do, but you did help her. You stopped him."

"But I let Reverend Felder cover the whole thing up. I should have called the police."

"And the good reverend would have blamed you. With Eddie to back him up, it would have been hard for you to not take the fall." Abe was really starting to hate the man. He had never been a fan of Reverend Felder. There was always something insincere and false about him. "You need to tell Harriet and Grandma Katie."

"No."

"They'll believe you—I know they will."

"And what can they do about it? It will only make trouble for them and piss Grandma Katie off."

"Then we'll have to try to find the girl and see what she remembers. Maybe she can help point the finger. If she remembers what happened, then she might need someone who'll back her up."

Lachlan nodded. "I'll do what I can to help her."

Abe released Lachlan, slid back behind the wheel, and put the truck in gear. "What did she look like?"

Lachlan groaned. "I know she had dark hair and was fairly tall. Pretty, with brown eyes. It's hard to describe someone when you've only seen them once." He turned away, looking out the window, and sighed. "She wore makeup, and it wasn't overdone…. She had a really nice purse. I don't think it was one of those knockoffs, but it could have been."

"Did she talk?"

"Yeah. A nice voice, very lyrical and rather soft, gentle." Lachlan shook his head. "That's all I can remember. I think the reverend knew her because he ushered her out and later said he'd taken her home. Maybe she goes to his church, or went there."

"Could you imagine going back there if she remembered what happened?" Abe shivered, wondering how she must have felt. "I need to say this again. You need to tell Harriet and Grandma Katie. They may be able to help us find her. If she went to the church, then Grandma Katie would know her."

Lachlan hummed softly. "I… I don't think I could take it if they didn't believe me."

"They will believe you, and I really think they could help us find her."

"Us?" Lachlan asked.

"Of course, us. Do you think I'm not going to help?" Abe wasn't sure if he was offended or not. "I know you'd never do anything to hurt anyone else, and if this girl needs someone to believe her, we'll do that too." He slowed and pulled into the drive. The back porch light was on, and Abe stopped near it, turning off the engine. "I know this isn't quite the date we had planned."

"It was nice. I loved the riding, and dinner was wonderful. Your friends Rory and Peter were so nice. I think I'll do my best to forget the rest and try to remember that."

Lachlan didn't open the door right away, and Abe leaned over, the bench seat rustling as he brought his lips to Lachlan's. The kiss was electric, and Abe deepened it. He could kiss Lachlan for the rest of his life and never get tired of it.

Instinct told him to push forward. Abe was rock hard, his pants way too damned tight. When he pressed to Lachlan, he felt a reciprocal hardness waiting for him. Knowing Lachlan wanted him in return only added to the excitement. He held Lachlan closer, breathing in his scent as he tasted his sweet lips.

The porch light flashed on and off, and Lachlan backed away, his cheeks reddening. Then he turned and opened the door to climb out of the truck. "Good night," Lachlan whispered, and Abe smiled as Lachlan touched his lips, climbed the stairs, and went inside. Only then did he go home.

CHAPTER 5

LACHLAN WOKE in the middle of the night gasping for air. It took him a while to calm down. He wasn't at home with his mother, nor was he at the Felders'. Somehow the death of his mother and things with Eddie had gotten mixed up and he'd dreamed Eddie was attacking his mother, but he didn't get there in time. It freaked him out until he could get it through his head that he was at Foster's, safe.

"Sweetie," Grandma Katie asked as she stuck her head in his room. "Are you all right?"

"Bad dream," Lachlan told her.

"Yeah. I still have those sometimes." She came in and sat on the edge of his bed the way his mother used to when he was younger. "I don't sleep so well anymore. It's one of the curses of getting old." She leaned toward him, as if sharing a secret. "Actually, most of the time it sucks. There are pains everywhere and in places you never knew you could hurt. But a good night's sleep is what I miss most." She patted his leg. "What's got you up?"

"My mom and…." *He* hadn't told them Eddie had been the one who drugged him yet. "Just a bunch of other things that got all mixed together."

"That happens to me too. When my son, Foster's dad, died, I started having dreams about my husband's death again. It's like stuff never goes away no matter how much we want it to."

"Does it get easier?" He kept seeing his mom all over the place, and it hurt like a wound whenever he thought about her.

"It does. But it never really goes away. You learn to deal with the loss, and sometimes the pain stays away for a while, but then you'll remember and it comes back." She leaned closer and lowered her voice to a whisper. "But it's the good times that stay with you. The

78

other things fade, but the love remains." She dabbed her eyes with her sleeve. "It's okay to grieve for your mom, but remember the good things. That will go a long way." She paused, and Lachlan wasn't sure if she had more to say or not. "But I think there's more to what's going on than just your mother."

"Did Abe say something?" Lachlan asked way too quickly.

"No. Of course not. If you asked him not to, then Abe never would. That boy is as trustworthy as the day is long. But you just confirmed what I thought. And I suspect it has something to do with what happened tonight." She patted his leg once again. "When you're ready to tell us, we'll listen. But if it had anything to do with Eddie Felder...."

Lachlan's gut clenched. Regardless of the guy being the biggest jerk in the county, Lachlan wasn't going to be believed or taken seriously. His mind raced ahead full steam as he geared up for yet another disappointment.

"It wasn't hard to figure out if you were staying with the reverend and then left suddenly. That boy is a bully, and his father needs to see him for who he really is."

Lachlan pulled his attention out of his own thoughts. "You'll believe me?"

Grandma Katie gave him a small nod. "Of course we will. If Eddie is causing trouble, then you need to speak up so we can try to help. Now, you think on that tonight and decide what you want to do." She slowly got to her feet and left the room.

When Lachlan lay back down and closed his eyes, he slept deeply for the first time in weeks.

THE FOLLOWING day, Lachlan was nervous all morning as he helped get the garden ready for planting and weeded the huge strawberry patch. At lunch he screwed up his courage and told the story of what had happened at the Felders', grateful that Abe sat next to him, holding his hand under the table. "I don't know who she is."

"I think I do," Grandma Katie said. "RaeAnn Lawson. She meets your description, and I know that the head of the Sunday school, Louise, was courting her to take over the third-grade class next year. She's a sweet girl, and she hasn't been in church for the last few weeks."

"That has to be her," Abe said, and Lachlan nodded.

"Do you know where she lives? Could you get her address through the church without anyone questioning why you need it?"

Grandma Katie grinned. "Of course. I'm on the Sunshine Committee. We visit shut-ins and send flowers when people lose someone, things like that. So I can ask for her address from the office or get it from her mailbox. I'll do it one way or another tomorrow." She shook her head. "The poor dear."

"Yeah." Not knowing what else to say, Lachlan pushed his chair away from the table and went back outside to finish the weeding.

The sun was warm on his back as he worked on his knees to pull the stubborn weeds that had already attached themselves between the strawberry plants. He kept his mind on the task in front of him rather than on what he was going to have to do tomorrow once Grandma Katie got home from church.

A pair of brown, scuffed boots appeared in Lachlan's line of sight. "You okay?" Abe asked.

"I don't know." Lachlan sat back on his haunches, and Abe knelt in front of him. "I'm glad Grandma Katie thinks she knows who Eddie hurt, but what do I tell her?"

"I don't know. I suppose you say what you'd want someone to tell you if you were in her position." Abe tugged him into his arms, and Lachlan went willingly. He needed someone steady at the moment. So much in his life had been in near-constant motion that having one person he could hold on to, have as his own, be his rock to cling to, was precious. "You know it's going to be okay."

"But what if she doesn't want to talk about it?" Lachlan asked, against Abe's shirt.

"Then that's okay too. She'll know you know and know you believe her. That alone has to help." Abe held him closer. Lachlan felt fragile at the moment, made of glass, and he was afraid that one more shock, another change, would shatter him. "You're strong and can handle anything."

Lachlan shook his head. That was the last thing he was, at least on the inside. "I'm scared to death half the time." Scared of losing the tentative home he had now. Scared of not being good enough. He walked on eggshells every single day, ensuring the people here wanted him.

"Is that why you didn't eat much at lunch?"

"I wasn't very hungry." His stomach rumbled, voicing loudly that he was now. Lachlan sighed, wishing he'd eaten when he had the chance.

Abe chuckled softly. "Go on inside. Grandma Katie probably put a couple sandwiches aside for you."

"Why?"

"She was raised on a farm and around hard work. If you aren't hungry, you will be soon. Work generates appetite, no matter how we feel or how nervous we are." Abe released him and took his hand to help Lachlan to his feet.

"Can I ask you something?" Lachlan fumbled, wondering how to ask what had been niggling at the back of his head. "You're always so nice to me, but you never do anything else. I mean, you kiss me sometimes, but you always stop and...." Lachlan looked down at the dark, sandy soil, giving it a kick. "You never do anything more, even after last night. We were dancing and we were close, and...."

"Are you asking why I haven't put the moves on you?"

"I guess so, yeah. I mean, if you're just being nice and aren't interested in that... then I understand." Lachlan turned away. He could hardly believe he'd actually brought up this topic of conversation. Maybe he should have just let things be. "I know. I should have kept quiet and just zipped my lip. Mom always said I would ask anyone anything, that I had a big mouth and should...."

Abe cut him off with a kiss, right there out in the open where anyone could see them. "I care for you, and every damn night I dream about you."

"You do?"

Cupping his chin, Abe looked him in the eye. "Damn right I do. But you're eighteen and I'm twenty-two. I know four years doesn't sound like a lot, but you have an amazing future ahead of you. You've been accepted to Michigan State and U of M, as well as half a dozen other colleges. You qualify for financial aid, and most of the colleges have offered you additional scholarships."

"Yeah, I know. I can get campus jobs for spending money and I should be okay...." Lachlan turned away.

"Then you need to choose where you're going to go, and we'll all make sure you're ready. You and your mom already did all the homework, so you're all set." Abe held him closer, strong arms winding around him. "I won't stand in your way. You could stay here and work on a farm for the rest of your life, milking cows and growing vegetables, or you can go to college and become the engineer you told me you wanted to be." His voice cracked a bit at the end.

"So you haven't done anything because you're afraid of what I'm going to choose?" Lachlan asked.

"No. I haven't done anything because you need to be the one to keep your options open, and I didn't want to pressure you. You deserve to be more than someone's roll in the hay. That's why I asked you out, and I want to go out with you again. I want us to be friends and...." Abe released him and turned away. "I want to be more than friends."

"Okay, then," Lachlan said, putting his hands on his hips. "I want that too. It's May and we have the entire summer." And a lot could happen between now and the start of school. "So maybe you and I can move things a little faster."

Abe groaned and shook his head. "How about we let things happen when the time is right?"

Lachlan was relieved when Abe moved back into his arms. "Okay. I can do that." He hugged Abe tightly. "But I have to tell you, I'm really horny."

Abe laughed. "I think I can feel that pretty well. Guys our age are always horny. And that's what gets most of us in trouble. And I want to treat you better than that. You deserve it."

"Why?"

Abe chuckled. "Because if anything happened and I broke your heart, I think Harriet and Grandma Katie would string me up by my nuts on their clothesline, and that's something I'd just as soon avoid. So let's just give ourselves some time." Abe gently cupped his cheeks and kissed him once again.

"If you two keep that up, no work is going to get done for the rest of the day," Javi teased as he made his way over.

Lachlan pulled away and went right back to work. He didn't want to upset anyone, and he didn't need Javi noticing that he was blushing to beat the band. Javi was right—he was supposed to be helping with the garden, not sucking face with Abe. "I'm sorry."

Javi touched his shoulder. "I was kidding. You two make each other happy, and that's nice to see." He knelt down next to him. "It's all right. We aren't a sweatshop or a forced labor camp." He patted his shoulder, and Lachlan stopped, raising his gaze. "I've seen both. Some of the places my family worked treated all of us like we were animals to be pushed and prodded until we nearly fell over with exhaustion. Others threatened to have us deported if we didn't work faster. They thought we were just chattel to be traded and treated any way they wanted. I will never, ever do that here."

"But there's plenty to do."

"Yes, and you've gotten nearly a day's work done already. The strawberry patch is looking really good, and next week, we'll plant the garden."

"I want to pull my weight." Lachlan saw Javi turn to Abe, who nodded and excused himself with a tiny wave.

"I know you're worried and you think that as soon as you make a mistake, we're going to throw you out. That isn't going to happen. Foster and I think of you as a younger brother. So relax a little and don't be afraid to have some fun." Javi turned to where Abe was heading into the milking room. "He's a good man and a hard worker."

"I know." Lachlan had trouble concentrating on things when Abe was around. "He makes me forget things sometimes, and I don't listen very well when he's around."

"I swear, when I first met Foster, I didn't pay attention to anything or anyone for the entire three weeks I was here with my family. So I'd say that's pretty normal when you're developing feelings for someone."

"But what about college? I think Abe is scared that I'm going to go away and never see him again." It was already hard for him to imagine wanting to spend time with other people the way he wanted to with Abe. He groaned. "I don't know what to do. He said he likes me and that he wants to take things slow because I deserve that."

"You know you do. We all do." Javi scratched his head. "There are basically two different kinds of guys. There are the ones like Eddie who feel that everyone is put on this earth for their pleasure, and hurting someone doesn't matter. Then there are guys like Abe. He cares enough about you to make sure you're happy, and when things do happen between you, it will be magical and special. Foster was pretty much the same way, and I'll take someone who cares about my feelings over what Foster once called a 'wham, bam, thank you, ma'am' kind of thing." He grinned widely. "Just give yourself a little time."

"I suppose you're right."

Javi sat on the ground, and Lachlan did the same. "It's easy when you've just lost someone to try to hold on to someone else. At first I went with my family. I felt I had to leave with them, but things didn't work out. When I left my family, I was lucky because I came here and I loved Foster."

"Did your family turn their back on you?"

"Pretty much. See, my brother, sister, and mother are out there, probably working fields somewhere, and I haven't seen or heard from any of them in months. I don't know if they're okay or anything, and I've had to get used to that. I'll admit it's been hard, and I'm lucky I've had Foster. He's been there the whole time."

"But I don't have anyone," Lachlan muttered, staring at the dirt spots on his knees.

"Yes, you do. You have all of us. We're all here for you." Javi gathered him in his arms, holding him, rocking slowly. "We aren't going to let you go."

Lachlan sniffed as the tears he'd held at bay for what seemed like weeks came to the surface. The loss of his mother and home swept over him. Lachlan clamped his eyes closed to try to stop the flood that he knew was coming. He quivered with the effort, then gave up, letting grief wash over him. He had to let it out. It was too strong, and no matter how much he'd tried to hold it in, the grief simply stayed put, waiting for a weak moment to come pouring out.

"That's it. Just let it go." Javi continued rocking, and Lachlan swallowed and nearly choked around his tears. He missed his mother with pain equal to losing a limb. It cut deeply and harshly through his heart and soul. Everything he'd known had been wrenched away from him, and as much as he might try to deny it, Lachlan was having a hard time getting his footing.

"Do you think I've been using Abe as some kind of replacement for my mom?" Lachlan asked, trying to get hold of himself. He couldn't believe he'd gone to pieces outside where anyone passing could see him, and part of him wanted to hide and retreat to someplace where he could be alone to nurse his grief and figure out the rest of his life.

"No," Javi answered gently. "I think that maybe you thought you needed someone to hold on to, and that's okay. We all need someone every now and then. I needed Foster after what happened with my family. And it's okay for you to need Abe, because he'll treat you right, and not everyone will."

"I want him to love me." Lachlan had no one at the moment. His mother had loved him and she was gone. It was funny to think how lonely he felt just thinking that there was no one who loved him. It was almost evil in the way it had eaten at him from within. "Someone has to."

Javi squeezed him tight. "And there will be plenty of people who will. You aren't alone. Foster and I care, and so do Harriet and Grandma Katie. We all care. Abe cares, maybe most of all."

Lachlan inhaled and moved back, wiping his eyes, using those few moments to hide so he could get his emotions back in order.

Abe came out of the milk room, and Lachlan knew almost instantly he was there. He hadn't seen him, but he lifted his head anyway and there he was, watching him. Lachlan had felt he was there without seeing him.

"Give yourself some time and don't make any huge decisions. You're welcome to stay here. We like having you, and in the fall, you'll go to school."

"But what if I want to stay?" Lachlan asked. He knew that wasn't the decision his mother would have wanted or necessarily what he wanted, but he had to ask.

"Then you'd be welcome. With the creamery—"

Lachlan's gaze shifted to the skeleton of the new building, its basic parts rising out of the ground, waiting for completion.

"—we'll need help. But you have a future ahead of you that's as big as the sky. You can do whatever you want in life. So don't sell yourself short. I didn't have those opportunities, and I sometimes wish I had. Not that I'm not happy here or that I don't love Foster with everything I am, but I didn't have choices, like you do."

"But you're smart. You could do whatever you wanted to do," Lachlan countered.

"Maybe. But my life is here with Foster, and I wouldn't give that up for anything."

"But what if my life is here with Abe?" Lachlan had to ask.

Javi didn't seem to have an answer for that right away. "Maybe that's true, and if it is, then he'll be here and that life will be here when you get back. The farm isn't going anywhere."

"But—"

"I don't have all the answers—no one does. All any of us can do is make the best decisions we can. I think you going to college and seeing that there is a whole big world out there just waiting for you is the best thing possible. You need to experience it and learn all you can. In the end you may return to the farm, but I suspect that once you see what's out there, the world will call you... somewhere."

"Where did the world call you?" Lachlan asked.

"It brought me to Foster, and I had to return here." Javi turned, and Lachlan followed his gaze to where Foster and Abe were standing together, talking to each other, their hands gesturing in sweeping arcs. They had to be going over the plans for the new building. "I wouldn't trade him or this place for anything in the world. This is my home, and I'd fight for it with my last breath." Javi took him by the hands. "I can't tell where you'll find your happiness, and maybe it's right here. But I do know it's something you have to find on your own. And I don't think you're going to find it here. Wait… that isn't what I mean. I don't think you're going to know if you found it unless you go out there"—he motioned around them—"and look."

"So I should go to school?"

"Most definitely, and you should experience life… all of it. The good and the hard. And if you find your heart drawn back here, we'll be waiting for you. I can promise you that."

"Okay…," Lachlan said, puzzled.

"Until then, try not to worry about everything. Life is a journey, and for some it seems like a constant uphill battle. If that's true for you, then fight the fight the entire way until you reach the top and figure out what will make you deliriously happy."

"But what about Abe?" Lachlan asked, still watching him in his jeans and light blue shirt. He knew the instant Abe saw him watching, a smile coming to his lips.

"That's an easy one. Just follow your heart." Javi squeezed his hand and stood. "I should get back to work or else things aren't going to be ready when we need them." The sun, which had been warm all morning and early afternoon, dimmed as a bank of clouds rolled in from the west. "Go ahead and finish up what you're doing."

Lachlan returned to his weeding, but his enjoyment faded. The spring weather changed quickly. The breeze picked up, carrying moisture and the heavy scent of rain. He hurried his pace, pulling as many of the weeds as he could to clear the patch as the temperature dropped. Lachlan kept warm because he kept moving and finished the weeding as the first drops of spring rain hit the earth around him. By the time he got his tools put away and the weeds dumped in one of the burn pits, the rain came down steadily, and he raced for the house.

"You have to be hungry now," Grandma Katie said as he came into the kitchen, shaking the water off his sleeves. "I heated up some chicken soup and made some tea." She already had a bowl on the table.

Lachlan sat down, his stomach rumbling as he ate quickly.

Grandma Katie joined him at the table. "I got RaeAnn's address."

"How?" he asked in between spoonfuls.

"I called the church and asked. The secretary gave it to me without a second thought." She handed him a piece of paper.

Lachlan stared at it as the blackness of what he'd seen washed over him once again.

"It's all right. You're doing the right thing by trying to help her."

Lachlan wondered what he'd do if she decided she didn't want his help, or worse, got angry with him. Then he wondered what he should do if RaeAnn wasn't the person he'd seen. At least he could thank her and walk away, but then they wouldn't be any closer to finding out who Eddie had been hurting. "Do you have her phone number?"

"Yes. I called and told her I wanted to pay her a visit. So finish your snack and you can drive me over."

"Now?" Lachlan's voice failed him, coming out as a whisper.

"Of course." She went back to work, and Lachlan's appetite left him once again. "You have nothing to be afraid of or nervous about."

"Who's nervous?" Abe asked as he came in and took the seat next to him. He bumped Lachlan's shoulder gently, and Lachlan couldn't help smiling.

"We're paying RaeAnn a visit," Grandma Katie said. She brought over some soup for Abe as well, and they ate.

Quietly, Lachlan said, "Abe, would you come too? I just need…."

Abe took Lachlan's hand, interlacing their fingers, nodding.

Knowing he had Abe's support, Lachlan's hunger returned, and he finished the chicken and vegetable soup, feeling less nerved up once he had something in his belly.

"Harriet," Grandma Katie said as she cleared the dishes. "The boys are taking me visiting."

"Do you want me to go as well?" Harriet asked as she came into the kitchen.

Grandma Katie answered before Lachlan could open his mouth. "I don't think she needs all of us descending on her, especially given the conversation we might be having." She went to the living room.

"Watch out for her," Harriet said as soon as Grandma Katie was out of the room. "She's slowing down, but she doesn't seem to realize it."

"Shame on you," Grandma Katie scolded when she returned, and Harriet rolled her eyes. "I can keep up with all you young whippersnappers." She was already heading for the door by the time Lachlan and Abe stood.

Harriet handed Lachlan the keys to her car, and Lachlan got Grandma Katie in, her black purse sitting on her lap over her deep purple dress. She held the handles of her purse, sitting straight up in her seat as though she were at a formal tea or something.

Lachlan buckled his seat belt and helped Grandma Katie fasten hers. Abe gently squeezed his shoulder, and Lachlan started the engine and pulled the tan sedan out of the drive, turning toward town. It wasn't hard to find the house as long as he tuned out Grandma Katie and Abe both giving him directions.

Finally he pulled to a stop and parked in the driveway of a small white house that looked like something out of a picture book. The beds in front were neat and tidy, and Lachlan imagined them waiting for a little more warmth before flowers burst into color. Even the walk and grass appeared to have been vacuumed as part of spring cleaning.

Lachlan stepped up on the concrete porch and rang the bell, trying not to bite his nails. He wasn't sure why he was so nervous. Then the door opened, and Lachlan was face-to-face with the woman from that night. She was a little older than he remembered because she wasn't wearing makeup, other than some light lipstick. There were bags under her eyes; clearly she hadn't been sleeping.

"RaeAnn, honey."

"Katie," she said softly and opened the door, holding it open for them to enter. "What brings you by?"

Grandma Katie turned to him, caution in her eyes, and then turned back to RaeAnn. "I noticed you haven't been in church, and I wanted to check that you were okay." She went inside, and Lachlan followed with Abe.

RaeAnn motioned them into a small but charming living room with painted furniture and warm floral prints. It was very much the home of someone with taste, and Lachlan wondered what a woman like this would ever have seen in Eddie. "I've been really busy and...."

As they passed the dining area, Lachlan noticed the table had been broken down and part of the room was filled with brown moving boxes.

"Sweetheart," Grandma Katie began in her best grandmotherly tone as she turned to Lachlan, whose mouth had gone completely dry. She sat on the edge of one of the chairs rather than settling back, and Lachlan did the same on the sofa, with Abe next to him. "We did miss you at church, very much, and I hope we see you back real soon, but that's not the only reason we're here."

"It isn't?" RaeAnn wrung her hands together.

"No." Lachlan found his voice, and looking into RaeAnn's almost haunted eyes, he knew he had to say something. "My mother died recently and I had no place to go, so the Felders took me in for a while."

Abe squeezed his hand, encouraging him.

"What Lachlan is trying to say is that he was staying at the house with Eddie Felder and...."

RaeAnn paled and looked about ready to pass out.

"I'm sorry, but I'm here because I saw what Eddie did," Lachlan said. "I didn't see very much, but I know he took advantage of you."

Her lower lip quivered and she sank onto a chair. "I wasn't sure if I imagined it or not. I remember being drowsy and Eddie offering me a drink of water. Then later I woke up and my clothes were a mess and Reverend Felder was sitting next to me, here in my living room. He told me I'd had too much to drink and passed out and he helped bring me home. But the last thing I remember is being at his house, and I don't think I had that much to drink, and...." She covered her face.

"It's all right, dear. This isn't your fault. Not at all." Grandma Katie was superb in the way she comforted her.

"I was upstairs in the room they let me use, doing my homework, and I came down for water. I don't know if Eddie remembered that I was in the house or not."

"Oh God. He lied to me, didn't he?" she asked, her voice muffled by her hands.

"Yes. He did, but I don't know how much." Lachlan wasn't sure how to put things, so he turned to Abe and Grandma Katie for help. "I doubt you drank very much, and it's more likely he put something into one of your drinks. We think he did that to me."

"He—" Her hands came away, her mouth hung open, and she widened her eyes in surprise.

"No. It was at the roller rink and he was trying to get to me. I think it was his way of threatening me so I wouldn't tell anyone what I saw. But with their help"—he gestured to Abe and Grandma Katie—"I realized I had to try to find you. I didn't know what you remembered, but I wanted you to know that I believed you."

She sighed. "I tried talking to Reverend Felder... and that was a huge mistake. He told me that women imagine things all the time, and that after he got home, he found me passed out and helped Eddie get me home. Then he suggested that I might need some substance abuse help and that he'd be willing to help counsel me."

"Yeah, well, when the good reverend found out I might have seen what Eddie did, he decided that I should find a different place to live." Lachlan slid closer to Abe. "I left on foot and was trying to get to the city because of him. I was lucky enough to find the farm."

"They're both...." She shivered. "I don't know what to say."

Grandma Katie shifted so she was next to her and held her. She turned to both of them, and Lachlan stood, pulling Abe with him.

They quietly left the house and stood under the porch roof to avoid the rain that had started, giving Grandma Katie and RaeAnn some time.

"Is this what you were afraid of?" Abe asked.

"I don't know. I just remembered when I came out of things yesterday that I wasn't sure what was real and what wasn't. So if Eddie used the same drug on her, she'd be confused, and now she knows that Eddie assaulted her. There's no confusion anymore. That also means that there's no place for her to hide." Lachlan shoved his hands in his pockets. "I wish that I'd never seen what I did."

"Yeah, but you know Eddie would still have taken advantage of her, and this way you stopped him."

Lachlan turned away. "How many other people has he done this to?" No sooner was the question out of his mouth than he wondered just how much the good reverend actually knew. "Do you think his dad has been helping him cover things up all along?"

Abe groaned. "He certainly knew how to play on RaeAnn's fears and make her think that everything was her fault. If nothing else, he's an enabler in the extreme."

They turned toward the door as it slid open, and Grandma Katie stood on the other side of the screen. She held the door open, and Lachlan and Abe went back inside. RaeAnn sat on her sofa, looking a little shell-shocked.

Lachlan walked up to her and sat down. "What do you want us to do?"

"Excuse me?" She blinked at him, eyes a little unfocused.

"I've been giving things some thought, and if you want to press charges, we'll back you up. I'll testify or talk to whoever you want me to."

She shook her head. "I'm going to move away and leave all this behind. I want to forget what happened and go on with my life."

Lachlan turned to Grandma Katie because he had no idea what to say. In his heart he didn't think that was right, but he didn't want to cause her any more pain. Eddie had already done enough of that.

"If that's what you want, dear, we won't bother you again." Grandma Katie stood. "But we'd hate to see you leave because of what one jerk did to you."

"What do you suggest I do, stand up in front of everyone and be the brunt of their jokes? Have them look at me like I'm a slut who let this happen to her?" Her eyes filled more with fear than anger.

"You're none of those things," Lachlan said.

Grandma Katie nodded slowly. "I'm willing to bet you're not the first girl he's done things like this to."

"The doctor Lachlan saw said there'd been a rise in drug cases," Abe added quietly.

"Oh God." RaeAnn placed her hands over her face. "What am I going to do?"

"Whatever you think is best," Abe told her gently. "Grandma Katie is going to give you her phone number, so please call if you need anything or if you want to talk. I know you probably don't want to talk to us guys, but she or Harriet will listen, and if you change your mind, we have your back."

She nodded slowly, like she was in pain, and Lachlan figured her world was falling in on her the same way he'd felt his was closing in around him after his mother died. "We should go." He stood and met Abe's gaze. He got up, and they left, going out to the car.

"We've done all we can, and Grandma Katie needs to be the one to try to help her. You and I are guys, and a guy did this to her. So I think talking to another woman might be helpful, and she isn't going to open up to us. Not that she's going to talk to her either, not right now. But maybe later."

"So what do we do? We can't let that slimeball get away with this."

"No." Lachlan turned to Abe, his jaw set. "He thinks he can use anyone he wants, and that has to stop. It's a pattern of behavior."

"True." They both slid into the car to get out of the rain.

"So there have to be more people he's hurt. And I bet there are more women. All we need to do is find them." Lachlan turned around to look at Abe in the backseat.

"And what are we going to do? Start asking anyone Eddie's dated if he drugged and assaulted them? We can't do that. You saw how torn apart she was. Can you imagine the others? If there are any."

"Then what do you suggest we do?" Lachlan turned back around, slumping in the seat. "Should we just let him get away with drugging me because he thought it was fun, or hurting her because he doesn't give a crap about anyone other than himself?"

"Of course not." Abe touched his shoulders. "I don't have the answers, but we have to be careful."

Lachlan sighed. "I know. It just sucks that he can do this stuff and get away with it because everyone is too scared to come forward."

"You don't seem to be any longer."

"But I can't prove what he did to me. It could have been anyone there, even though we know that's crap. We can help RaeAnn if she comes forward, but if she doesn't, then I'm only stirring up trouble." He hung his head, looking down at his feet. "I don't know what to do."

Abe got out and opened the door for Grandma Katie to get in the passenger seat, then got back in. Lachlan started the engine and pulled away from the house, driving carefully.

"That poor girl. She's scared of her own shadow right now." Grandma Katie squeezed his arm. "What you did for her was pretty brave."

"I wish I could do more." Lachlan pulled to a stop at an intersection. "What do you think she'll do?"

"I don't know. Only time will tell. Right now she's feeling like a victim, which makes her want to run and hide, and I can't blame her." Grandma Katie sat with her purse clutched in front of her. "But I do know that I want to wring the reverend's neck. I don't know if I can set foot in that church again."

"Of course you can," Lachlan said with a grin. "And when you do, you can hint to the Reverend Felder that you know what Eddie has been up to and what he did to cover it up." God, he felt evil… in the best way possible.

"A sort of 'I know what you did' kind of thing," Abe said.

"Yes. Tell him that you had the most interesting talk with someone who Eddie dated."

"Boys. Do you really think that's my style?"

Lachlan hesitated for two seconds and answered at the same time as Abe did. "Yes."

She laughed. "You better believe it." Grandma Katie sat back in her seat, grinning. "You know, I don't think I've looked forward to going to church this much in years."

Lachlan expected her to rub her hands together maniacally as he made the turn onto the road that led out to the farm.

CHAPTER 6

"HEY, ABE, get your head out of the clouds," Foster said, and Abe shook his head, pulling his attention back to the present. "What's going on, besides Lachlan?" Foster winked at him.

"Nothing. He's been pretty quiet, and I'm a little worried."

"I get that. But he's been through a lot. Just give him a little time." Foster attached the length of siding to the pole building, which was really starting to take shape. Apparently he'd negotiated a price reduction as long as he chipped in on the labor.

"I know. But…."

Foster finished what he was doing and turned toward him. "He's got a lot going on right now and things are compounding. The whole thing with Eddie and trying to help RaeAnn is only adding to it."

"What do I do?" Abe turned to where the object of his fascination was bent over in the garden, working with Javi to get seeds in the ground.

"The two of you have been pretty inseparable for the last two weeks, even if he's being quiet. So I really don't see the issue." Foster returned to what he'd been doing. "Don't beg trouble and just go with the flow."

"But I only have so much time."

"Is that what's bothering you?" Foster asked. "You feel that this relationship has a time limit on it? He's about to graduate from high school, and thanks to help and prodding from you and Mom, he's going to Michigan State in the fall. It isn't like Lansing is a world away. It's less than a hundred miles."

"But he'll meet a lot of people more interesting than me." Abe sighed.

Foster laughed. "Yeah, he probably will. But none of them will touch his heart the way you have. So stop worrying about what might happen. He's here now, and you can't let the fear of the future stop you from actually having one. Now pull your head out of your butt and give me a hand with this." He gestured to another section of siding, and Abe hoisted it up and held it while Foster fastened it into place.

Between milkings, Abe worked with Foster and the guys from the construction firm to finish putting up the pole building. The doors just needed to be hung before it was ready to go.

"When do you think you'll start the creamery operation?" Abe asked as he and Foster completed the evening milking.

"I have some equipment ordered, which will arrive in the next week. Lachlan, Javi, and Grandma Katie have been working to perfect some recipes for ice cream, and Grandma Katie says she found some cheese processes that her mother used. I thought it would be great to start there and see what happens. The farmer's market really begins in earnest by mid-June, and I'd like to have something to sell by then, but that's probably pushing it." Foster turned to survey their handiwork, and Abe did the same.

"I'm sure Javi and Lachlan will have something. They've had their heads together making plans over the past few weeks." It had been the only time Lachlan had gotten truly excited about anything. Suddenly Abe turned and hurried toward the house.

"Where are you going?" Foster asked as Abe veered off toward the garden.

"I just thought of something." He ran to where Lachlan and Javi were looking over rows and rows of vegetables, each marked with stakes and labels. As he approached, Javi nudged Lachlan, and Abe got the idea that the two of them might have been having a conversation similar to the one he'd just had with Foster.

"I was wondering if you might want to have dinner tonight?" Abe asked Lachlan.

"Go have some fun," Javi said with another nudge.

"Are you sure? There's still some things to plant."

"We're almost done, and what little is left, I can handle." Javi brushed off his hands. "Go on and get changed."

Lachlan hurried toward the house with more spring in his step than he'd had in weeks.

Javi smiled. "It's nice to see him excited."

"I know."

"He's running scared. College and graduation, all the things most people do, have him worried sick." Javi sighed. "He hasn't said anything, but I think he's afraid that once he leaves, there isn't going to be a place for him to come home to."

"But there is…," Abe prompted. As far as he was concerned, Lachlan was developing a permanent home in his heart. Abe knew it, and that scared him as well. What was he going to do if Lachlan went away and met someone else? Abe tried to put that out of his mind.

"Of course. He'll have a place here as long as he wants it."

The bigheartedness of everyone here sometimes blew him away. His own father would never open himself and his home up like that.

"Then how do we help him understand that?"

"He will. See, what I think Lachlan needs is a home—not one that comes from a building or land, but from the people engaging his heart." Javi pulled his gloves back on and turned toward the last section of the garden. "Take him out and show him what he could have."

Abe nodded and hurried to his truck. He raced home and up the stairs to the bathroom to shower. Thankfully his father was out for the evening. Once he'd cleaned up and changed, he hurried back downstairs and nearly collided into Randy.

"I took your advice."

"Oh yeah? Awesome."

"Foster said he's starting a creamery at the farm." Randy folded his arms over his chest. "You didn't say anything about that when we talked."

"It wasn't my news to share."

"He said that if it gets going, he'd like to buy some of our milk for the creamery." Randy's gaze softened. "And he said that if

98

things work out, he could pay more than the dairy we deal with now." Randy's expression made it hard for Abe to decipher his thoughts at the moment. "He also said that we could sell our eggs at the market." Now, finally, Randy smiled. "He's something else."

"I know." Abe headed for the door. "I have to go. I have a date."

"With a guy?"

"Yes," Abe answered cautiously. His brother was cool with him being gay, but he wasn't sure how much he really wanted to know.

"Do you guys really do that or is that some kind of euphemism?"

Abe put his hands on his hips, stepping forward. "First thing, I'd have thought that a word like 'euphemism' was a little outside your maximum two-syllable vocabulary. And yes, we date. Jesus, there's no need to be a complete jackass."

Randy stepped back and held up his hands. "Hey. I was just asking. How would I know about things like that between guys?" He seemed surprised at Abe's anger. "Being a little sensitive?"

Abe rubbed the back of his neck. "Maybe. I like this guy, and all he and I have done is kiss, okay? I told you about him before."

Randy smiled. "The jailbait." Abe growled, but Randy laughed. "I'm just yanking your chain." He turned toward the living room, peering out the window. "As it happens, I have a date of sorts too, and Dad was supposed to be back so I could go." Randy glanced out the window once more. "Have fun."

Abe said he would before hurrying out of the house. He wasn't particularly interested in running into his dad at the moment. Staying out of his way seemed the best possible option. He left and saw his father's truck on the road as he went, waving as they passed.

Lachlan was ready when he arrived, and he climbed into the truck. "Where are we going?"

"I thought we'd run into town to get something to eat." Abe had every intention of getting their food to go. He wasn't going to take any chances on a repeat of the situation with Eddie. He wanted this evening to be special, and he was determined to make it that way. He started the truck and pulled out of the drive, heading to town.

Twenty minutes later, with containers of egg salad and bread in a bag on the floor, Abe headed to overlook point. The steep ascent of one of the local sand hills led to a breathtaking view from the top, overlooking the entire area. Abe was grateful that the small area was deserted, since there was only room enough for about two cars. He had been up here before, but never with someone he cared for. He turned the truck so the back had the best view and killed the engine.

"Grab the food, okay?" Abe asked, reaching behind the seat to find the stadium cushions. Then he got out and walked around back, lowered the tailgate, and set out the cushions with the food between them. "I used to come here sometimes when I wanted to think." He sat and waited for Lachlan to do the same, then pointed. "There's our farm, and that's Foster and Javi's."

"You always refer to it that way, but isn't the farm really Harriet's?" Lachlan asked.

"I suppose it is. But I think of it as Foster and Javi's because if it weren't for them, there wouldn't be a farm. Foster's dad left it in pretty bad financial shape. Foster and Javi turned it around." Abe pulled out the sodas and started laying out the food and bread, flattening the bag to use as a tabletop before opening the containers.

The sun would start to set soon, already bathing the wispy clouds with tinges of yellow and orange, and the lights would start to come on down below. It was a beautiful sight.

"Grandma Katie got a call from RaeAnn today," Lachlan said. "She's decided to go to the police and file a complaint and asked if it would be okay if she named me as a witness. I told Grandma Katie to tell her yes. It makes me nervous, but I know it's the right thing to do." He scooped some egg salad onto a piece of bread and began munching.

"You're doing the right thing, and once one person comes forward, maybe others will too." Abe hoped that was true, or Lachlan and RaeAnn would be standing up against the reverend and Eddie alone. Granted, they were in the right, but some people would believe the reverend no matter what he said. "I'll be here. I have your back."

Lachlan reached over to take his hand. "I know you do." Lachlan squeezed and leaned over the food. Abe did as well, and their lips met tenderly, but with such heat that the cool evening air didn't stand a chance. Lachlan tasted of the seasonings from the food mixed with his own underlying sweetness. Abe could do this forever if Lachlan would let him.

When they broke apart, Lachlan blushed the way he normally did, but not as red as usual. It was adorable. He returned to eating, and Abe did the same. After a full day of work, they were both hungry, and the food didn't last very long. Abe gathered the empty containers and put them all in the bag, then set the whole mess behind them in the truck bed.

The air was blessedly still, and Abe was grateful. This time of year, even though the temperature was moderate, a breeze could be chilling. Early spring was beautiful, with all the flowers and trees in bloom, but the weather could be unpredictable. Today nothing marred the bright blue sky.

Abe scooted his seat closer to Lachlan's, looking out over his home. "I've lived here all my life, but I used to dream about leaving and seeing the rest of the world."

"Then why didn't you?"

It was a natural question, and one Abe didn't have an answer for that didn't sound a little lame. He shrugged. "Dreaming about something is good, but reality is a whole different ball game. I need to make a living, and it isn't like I have skills that will take me anywhere. I understand dairy farming because it's what I've done all my life. But it isn't like I can just go out and buy a farm on a whim. The land is too costly, with pressure put on it by development in surrounding areas. Starting my own farm anytime soon isn't really viable... so I work for someone else and do my best to save. It was either that or stay at home and work for free for my father, who doesn't listen to anyone. At least Foster listens to what I have to say, and once the pole building is done, we're going to build a hutch and see if we can develop a market for rabbit."

Lachlan shivered. "I know it's just meat, but the thought of eating bunnies gets to me."

"It's really good, and there are restaurants that have it on the menu now. If its locally raised, that's a plus that we can use." He really needed to change the subject because it seemed to weird Lachlan out. "The point is that Foster liked my idea, and if the creamery takes off, it looks like Foster will be able to help my dad and Randy."

"That's good, then."

"Really good. If Foster needs more milk for the creamery and he's willing to pay a little bit more than the standard milk distributor, then we all win, and it helps push the price up for everyone. We're all interconnected, and if one of us is doing well, it helps everyone else." Abe chuckled. "I think that's enough shop talk." He grabbed a napkin and wiped a small dab of salad dressing off Lachlan's upper lip before kissing him again.

The world around them fell away as Lachlan's soft lips trembled against his. Abe leaned closer, holding Lachlan, steadying him as he deepened the kiss. Abe's ears buzzed a little and he realized it was the blood racing through his veins, excitement building in him. He and Lachlan had been circling around each other in this weird dance where Abe wanted to be sure that he wasn't pressuring Lachlan, and now it seemed Lachlan was more than a little interested in being pressured.

"I like it up here," Lachlan said when they separated a few seconds later. "It's quiet and so private." He clung to Abe, kissing with what felt like a touch of desperation and a lot of passion. Lachlan leaned into him, pressing him back into the bed of the truck. Abe hadn't been expecting this kind of aggression, and, damn, did it feel amazing. To be wanted… desired… like this was mind-spinning, and when Lachlan lay on top of him, squirming and grinding against him, Abe nearly went off like a rocket.

"I do too." Abe gasped for breath, trying to gain some kind of control over his errant body, which seemed to have developed a mind of its own. Not that he intended to tell Lachlan to stop, but if they kept things up, it was going to be all over and he would end up with a squishy mess in his pants.

Lachlan felt like he belonged in Abe's arms, and Abe held him closer, sliding his hands down to the curve of his back and then over his butt, which fit perfectly in his hands. It could have been raining cats and dogs and he wouldn't have cared. All that mattered was Lachlan's weight pressed on him and the intense electricity that passed through Abe whenever Lachlan kissed him.

"This is so incredible."

He slid his fingers under the waistband of Lachlan's pants, testing the waters to see if going further was okay. Lachlan groaned and thrust his hips forward, grinding against Abe with more energy. It seemed Lachlan wanted him as badly as he did Lachlan.

Lachlan shifted and reached for the buckle of Abe's jeans, yanked it open, and went for the button. As soon as the pressure eased, Lachlan tugged the fabric apart and reached into his briefs. Abe moaned and gritted his teeth as Lachlan's fingers touched him. When they closed around his shaft, Abe was instantly on the edge, thinking unsexy thoughts to keep from going off and embarrassing himself. Somehow he managed to make his fingers work and reciprocate, getting Lachlan's pants open, and damn…. Lachlan was a handful, and that sent him over the edge, with Lachlan following right behind him.

Abe lay still, afraid to move, not wanting this feeling of elation to fade for a second.

"Was that okay?"

Abe chuckled. "It was amazing." He tugged his hand away from Lachlan and found a napkin, then wiped his hand before holding Lachlan tight, kissing him deeply. "You're incredible, you know that?"

"I don't think so," Lachlan said breathily before slowly getting up. Abe handed him a napkin and got a few more, cleaning himself up and fixing his pants before sitting up. Lachlan did the same, and they sat together on the tailgate.

"What do you want more than anything in the world?" Abe asked, an arm around Lachlan because he couldn't bear to let him go for a second.

"I don't know. I used to dream about being able to travel. My mom went to Europe when she was in high school as part of a class trip and she used to tell me all about it. I used to dream about going there to see some of the things she described, like the Eiffel Tower and St. Paul's Cathedral. They always sounded so amazing. But all that will have to wait until after I'm done with school. I think it's like you said—sometimes practical matters have to take precedence."

"Yeah. But we still need dreams. I wanted to travel too, and now my dream is to have a place of my own, someday. I know I won't get the family farm, so I'd like to start my own, but that takes a lot of money. So I try to save a little, and hopefully before I'm dead I'll be able to have some land of my own. But I know it will take a long time."

"I know. Sometimes dreams seem so far out of reach that it isn't worth bothering with them. Right now I want to get through each day as it comes." Lachlan turned to him. "Have you ever felt like you're stuck in mud and it keeps getting deeper and deeper? All you want to do is get out, but whenever you make some progress, you get pulled right back."

"Yeah. After my mom died. Dad was little help. He was deep in his own grief, and maybe he still is. I don't know. The dad I had growing up isn't the one I have now. He's cold and distant, and he wasn't like that when Mom was alive."

"Maybe your dad has forgotten how to live." Lachlan tilted his head. "I think that's happening to me sometimes. I don't want to forget her, so I spend a lot of time remembering and thinking of her. But she isn't here, so that makes me sad, and I want her back." He wiped his eyes. "I really want her back more than anything in the world. Her love was unconditional. It didn't matter if I messed up sometimes. She loved me no matter what and she always will."

"My mom used to say that when someone loves you, really loves you, that love never ends. When they die, their love stays with you."

Abe swallowed hard and wiped his own eyes. "I believe her. Because I carry my mom with me, and I know you carry yours too."

Lachlan nodded slowly.

"But we can't stop living or dreaming because they're gone."

"No. My mom would be angry with me if I gave up on everything she wanted for me. You saw our apartment. Mom and I didn't have much, but she made sure I never wanted for anything, and she was so determined to give me a better life than the one she had. So I'm going to go to college and be the best student I can. I'm going to be an engineer of some sort."

Abe pulled Lachlan closer. That idea hurt as well as made him happy. He was pleased that Lachlan was going to go to college and make the most of his life, but he didn't want him to go away. He wanted Lachlan to stay here with him, and those two ideas tore at him. He was determined to keep quiet about it because going to college was the right thing for Lachlan. "That's what you have to do. You'll find your future, and it's going to be bright and filled with promise." He had no doubt about that. But as Abe tried to look into Lachlan's bright future, he saw himself fading from it. He wasn't going to hold Lachlan back, as much as he wanted to tighten his arms around him and keep him here forever. That wasn't the right thing to do. Still, as Lachlan sat next to him, Abe could feel the wings on his back already starting to sprout, and soon they'd mature and Lachlan would fly away into his future, leaving him behind.

Lachlan turned to him, leaning close to kiss him. The doubts, worries, and Abe's ability to think all flew away when Lachlan kissed him. "I'm really starting to like it up here."

The lights came on one by one down below as the sun dipped below the horizon.

"Me too," Abe agreed, paying no attention to the map laid out below them as Lachlan turned back to him, eyes darkening to the point that Abe could get lost in them. The truth was that he'd go just about anywhere to be close to Lachlan.

A breeze blew through the scrubby brush nearby, accentuating the dropping temperatures. Lachlan shivered, and Abe gathered up the trash and slid off the tailgate. "It's probably time we headed back." They should have brought jackets, but Abe hadn't thought of that. It had been warm enough earlier not to need them. He waited for Lachlan to hop down before raising the tailgate. Then they climbed into the cab, and Abe carefully drove back down to level ground. He wasn't ready to take Lachlan home, so he headed for town.

The Happy Cow ice cream stand had just opened for the season. Abe pulled in, and they got in line. Lachlan looked all around and relaxed. Abe had checked to make sure Eddie was nowhere in sight as well.

"What do you want?" Abe asked when they were nearly at the window.

"The black raspberry," Lachlan answered, and when their turn came, Abe placed their order, getting dark chocolate for himself. They took their cones and sat in the truck with the doors open to eat. "This is good, but there's something…." Lachlan tasted it again. "It's got a slight chemical taste. They're using flavorings instead of all real fruit." He offered Abe a taste, and he had to agree. There was something off about it. Abe offered his, and they agreed that it was much better. "There's real chocolate in here. This isn't just flavor."

"What are you thinking?"

"That I have to talk to Foster and Grandma Katie. If he wants to do ice cream, then all the flavors have to be real, from real fruit, not flavorings." Lachlan finished his cone and went to throw away the trash.

Abe saw a familiar car pull in and motioned Lachlan back. He hurried inside, and Abe backed out of their spot as Eddie sauntered up to the window. They were gone and on their way back to the farm before he saw them.

"You know it's going to get worse with him just as soon as RaeAnn comes forward."

"I know," Lachlan said with remarkable ease. "But this has to happen, and if I can help, I will. I'm determined that he isn't going to hurt anyone else."

Abe knew Lachlan was going to need all his convictions for what would come.

Abe pulled into the drive, parked near the house, and turned off the engine. He sat staring out the windshield at the pen of cows ahead of him.

"Are you okay?" Lachlan whispered. "Do you regret what happened?"

Abe gasped and turned. "No. It just seemed strange to let you go." He hoped no one was watching as he leaned over to take Lachlan in his arms. Their kiss was explosive. Abe hadn't intended for it to be so intense, but it just happened, and Lachlan pulled him down until they were both lying on the bench seat, rubbing against each other.

The porch light flashed on and off, and Abe groaned.

Lachlan humphed and then broke out into laughter. "Ten to one it's Grandma Katie. She's been watching us and just waiting for things to get good."

"That's so wrong in so many ways." Abe sat up and straightened his clothes. "First thing, I don't want an audience. And second, I love her to death, but thinking of a grandma watching us get... well... busy, is really drooptastic, if you know what I mean."

"Yeah. I get that." Lachlan checked his clothes and opened the truck door. "I'll see you tomorrow." He leaned in for a quick kiss and then closed the truck door and walked through the headlight beams before going inside.

Abe waited until he was gone before pulling out and driving the short distance home.

The lights were on in one of the outbuildings that housed some of the equipment, and he walked over to see what was up. "Hey, Randy," Abe said to his brother's legs.

Randy slid out from under the tractor, grease streaked on his cheeks. "I got this thing fixed, I hope to God. But I don't know how long it's going to stay that way. The damn thing is wearing out, and we can't afford to replace it. Not now anyway."

"Do you need my help?"

"No. There's nothing any of us can do except pray the repair lasts the season and that we have a really good year." He started the engine, and the tractor sounded normal to Abe. Randy turned it off again and climbed down. "I started work on an enlarged chicken coop. The girls are really laying right now, and Mrs. Laramie has an abundance of chicks. She gave me two dozen because she doesn't know what she's going to do with them all. Apparently the kids didn't keep the rooster under control and he fertilized the eggs, so her choice was to destroy them or let them hatch. I helped her out with feed and things for them in exchange."

"That's awesome! Her chickens are great stock and terrific layers."

"I talked to Foster, and he said he'd take the eggs to market for us and we'd split the proceeds. It means we'll make a decent price per dozen and it'll be some cash. We'll start small and see how it goes."

"I think it's fantastic. We need something that will generate ready cash, and eggs could be it. Foster did it with produce. I think eggs is a great start."

Randy nodded. "I'm also going to fence off the south pasture and bring in a couple dozen beef cattle. We're used to raising milk cows, but we could produce our own beef and have it butchered and sell that as well. Like you said, we can see how it goes."

"Now you're thinking. Milk prices rise and fall and we're always at the mercy of the market. We used to be able to make ends meet with the milk, but sometimes the price is just too low and we're screwed."

"Diversification." Randy smiled.

"Exactly." They high-fived each other and then laughed. It had been quite a while since they had shared something to celebrate. "What does Dad say?"

Randy rolled his eyes. "He wasn't in favor, but I told him that since I put my money into the farm to help bail it out, that my business ideas had to be considered. He doesn't want anything to change."

"Yeah. I chatted with Lachlan today. We talked about losing our mothers, and it struck a chord with me. I think Dad is still missing Mom. He doesn't want anything to change because then he loses another part of her." Abe stood still, watching as Randy nodded, some of the light leaving his eyes.

"I still miss her," Randy admitted, then turned before walking to the tool bench in the back of the shed, putting everything away... loudly. He kept his back to him, and Abe contemplated going to talk to him, but the banging increased, followed by a slam of metal on the bench.

Abe, deciding to give him some space, walked to the other shed and pushed the door open before turning on the light. His motorcycle stood under a tarp, and he pulled the cover off. It was fairly clean but definitely looked neglected. Abe stared at it, falling into his own thoughts, and didn't hear footsteps behind him.

"You going to work on that?"

"Yeah. Lachlan likes motorcycles and understands engines, so I think we're going to do it together." He turned and caught Randy nodding.

"I think it's time we bring everything back to life here. We've all been frozen—Dad, me, you, the farm. Mom passed away, and we've been hanging on and hoping that something would change. But it's not going to happen unless we make it."

"You know, Mom would be pissed as hell if she saw things the way they are now." Abe checked the tires and figured he'd need to get new ones since these had been sitting for so long. "She always liked things bright and cheerful." He smiled wide. "So let's do it. And maybe we can go through the house and clear out some of the clutter."

"Yeah, and maybe it's time we both move on with other areas of our lives. You seem to be trying."

"I am. I think you should too." Abe patted Randy on the shoulder. "Find yourself a nice girl, or a naughty one, whichever type you prefer.... It would be a girl, right?" He couldn't resist the tease.

"Yeah.... But nearly everyone in this town feels like a sister or something. I went to school with a lot of them. It doesn't feel right somehow. But like I said, I did have a date."

Abe nodded. "If she seems too sisterly," he teased, "you could try online dating. Or go into Muskegon or Grand Rapids to meet people. You could start going to church, but stay away from the one on Main where Felder preaches."

"Why?" Randy raised an eyebrow.

"There's going to be trouble coming. Plenty of it."

Randy rolled his eyes. "What has Eddie been up to now, and how do you know about it?"

"I'm not starting any rumors, but if the church girl type is your cup of tea, just pick a different church to shop at." Abe laughed at his little joke. "Seriously, find someone who will make you happy. I'm certainly trying."

Randy's expression hardened for two seconds and then he smiled. "When am I going to get to meet this guy?"

"Soon. Once the planting and spring work is done, I'm hoping we can start on the bike, and he'll be by."

"Good." Randy leaned against the doorway. "Do you plan to stay out here all night?"

Abe tossed the cover back over the bike. "I was hoping I could wait until Dad went to bed. He and I don't see things the same way at all and we just seem to argue."

"Maybe we all need to give each other a break. If what you say is true, then maybe Dad is just as lost as we all seem to be."

Abe laughed until he began coughing.

"Okay…." Randy narrowed his eyes. "What's gotten into you?"

"Maybe he needs to go to church and meet a woman. He isn't that old, and he shouldn't be alone for the rest of his life."

Randy put his hands up instantly. "I tried telling him that once, and he nearly bit my head off, saying that he didn't want to forget Mom."

Abe looked up at the house and in through the kitchen window, where their father moved between the sink and the table in the same robe he'd had for years, the one their mother had given him for Christmas that last year. Why Abe had never seen it before was a shock, but they were right. They had all been stuck in the past, and in an offbeat way, Abe had Lachlan to thank for opening his eyes. Now all he needed to do was figure out how he was going to do something about it. "Come on. Let's go on in. I could use a drink."

"Amen to that. There's beer in the fridge."

Just what the doctor ordered. It had been a long time since he and Randy had had a beer together.

CHAPTER 7

"PASS ME the wrench, please," Lachlan said as he held the other end of the fuel line. The few months he'd spent working at a garage that specialized in motorcycles before he and his mother moved was paying off. Granted, this was an older, much simpler engine than the ones used today. Abe put the tool in his hand, and he got the other end free. Sitting up, he blew through it and knew it was clogged. "We need to clean this out. There was a small amount of fuel left in it, and it got really cruddy over the years."

"All right. What about the spark plugs?"

"I already replaced them and cleaned out the rest of the fuel system. This should be the last of it, and once I finish this, with any luck, this baby will start." Lachlan set to work, gently cleaning out the line. They could try to get a new one, but keeping as many parts original was best. Of course, if the fuel line was really badly plugged, they'd have to. Lachlan got some crud out and continued working until it seemed clear and he was able to pass air through it. Then he cleaned it as best he could and decided to soak it in some solvent for a while to get out any residual deposits. "What about the paint?"

"I've been thinking about that. It's pretty worn and scuffed."

"Let's get it running and see what else we need to do. You could check the brakes while I'm finishing this up. Make sure you have some. It would be pretty bad if you got this bad boy up to speed and couldn't slow down." Lachlan smiled. It was fun having a project to do with Abe. "The seat is pretty worn as well."

"I don't suppose you know how to upholster?" There was a twinkle in Abe's eye.

Lachlan sat up, putting his hands on his hips. "I do. I repaired the seats in my mother's car once. But I think we should find someone who can do this right or see if we can locate a used seat that's in better condition." He suspected the time in the barn had been terrible on the leather, which was brittle and wasn't going to hold together with any use.

Abe checked on the brakes and determined that they needed to be replaced. He also inspected the hand controls, which seemed to be working. "It looks like we'll need to wait to take a spin even if we get the engine running. I was hoping for a short ride."

"Me too." But they couldn't do anything about it now. One step at a time. Lachlan got the cleaned-out fuel line ready and hooked it up again. Then he added a small amount of fresh fuel to the tank and stood back while Abe got on and tried to get it started. The first time— nothing. "Try one more time," Lachlan said, knowing it would take a little effort to get the fuel through the empty system.

Abe tried a few more times and then the engine rumbled throatily to life.

Lachlan fisted the air, grinning like an idiot as the engine kept running. It wasn't safe to take the bike on the road, but getting the engine going again was a major step forward. "Okay, shut it down," Lachlan said. Once the engine was quiet, he grabbed a pencil and pad off the workbench and began making a list of the rest of the work that needed to be done.

"What's all the commotion?"

"Lachlan, this is my brother, Randy."

Randy extended his hand and Lachlan shook it.

"We're making real progress on the bike."

"So I heard." Randy passed the door frame. "Keep up the good work. I was beginning to think we'd need to use it for a doorstop." Randy grinned, and Abe flipped him off with a smile. Shaking his head, Randy turned and left.

"I can't believe we got it running already," Abe said, throwing his arms around Lachlan's neck and bringing him in for a kiss that was hotter than a pulsing piston.

Lachlan closed his eyes and pushed into the embrace. His heart raced and his brain raced down the road of possibilities, forgetting where they were. Then he heard a throat clearing, followed by a growl so menacing, Lachlan didn't know a human could make that sound.

"I see the evidence of my son's perversion right in front of me."

Lachlan squeaked and pulled away, out of Abe's arms, like he'd been shot. He tried to get up, but his foot caught a slick of oil and flew out from under him. Lachlan ended up on his butt, squeaking again like some small fucking mouse. "I'm Lachlan, and I—"

"I know who you are." Though he hadn't met Abe's father yet, this huge man with graying hair and a voice with tones of thunder looked like an older version of Abe. There was no doubt who he was. "And I know you perverted my son."

"Excuse me, Dad. I'm gay and you know that." Abe stepped forward, standing between Lachlan and his dad like a wall as Lachlan tried to get to his feet. "Lachlan is special to me, and you need to treat him that way." The resonance in Abe's voice would have been sexy under other circumstances. "So quit this perversion stuff."

"I will not. And I'm not talking about him being gay. He's accusing the reverend of hurting some girl, and there's no way that's the truth. Reverend Felder is a good man, and it's his job to show us the way to salvation. He'd never hurt anyone." He glared at Lachlan until a shiver ran up his spine. "How dare you lie like that to the police, to the entire town...."

Lachlan stepped back as anger filled the shed.

"You need to leave and never set foot on my property again." His hand pointed with a single finger, which reminded Lachlan of the Ghost of Christmas Yet to Come, and it felt just as ominous.

Abe looked at him, and Lachlan shrugged. He didn't know where any of this was coming from. He hadn't talked to anyone about the reverend since they'd spoken with RaeAnn.

"That's enough, Dad. Eddie Felder assaulted someone, and his father helped cover it up. Lachlan was there—he saw what happened."

"Exactly. He stayed with them. The reverend provided him with a home when he didn't have one, and this is how he repays him, with lies and—"

"It's not a lie. Eddie Felder is a menace and a bully. He thinks that because his father is the all-powerful reverend that he can get away with anything he wants. Look at you!" Abe stepped closer to his father, tossing a hand in his direction. "You have no idea what the facts are, but you're taking the reverend's word just because you think you know him. Well, you have no idea."

Lachlan was a small boat caught on a sea of their anger, and he wanted to get away as fast as he could. But he wasn't going to leave Abe, not when he was standing up for him.

"I don't—"

"No. Have you stopped to think the kind of guts it took for Eddie's accuser to come forward? Or how the whole town is going to give her grief? Lachlan is standing up to say what he saw because it's the right thing to do. It's what you and Mom taught me. You both always said to do what's right, and when someone does that, you decide you know better." Abe put his hands on his hips. "Mom would be ashamed."

The slap of skin on skin echoed off the walls of the shed, and Abe's father stood stock still, his hand in midair. Abe's cheek blossomed red, and yet neither of them moved. "Jesus...," Abe's father groaned and then turned and walked toward the house without another word.

"Mr. Armitage," Lachlan called. He had to try to salvage things between Abe and his father if he could. "How did you know I was the witness? No one called me."

"The reverend told me it had to be you," he called without turning back.

"If nothing happened, then how did he know?" Lachlan called, and Abe's father stopped in his tracks. "Why do you think the good reverend decided on a dime that he needed to get me out of his house? He tried to tell me that I dreamed what I saw." He stood at the door of the shed. "But I saw Eddie assault that girl, and I won't back down because the reverend is trying to turn everyone against her and me. I know what I saw."

Abe's father didn't move for a few seconds, and Lachlan hoped he'd see reason, but then he continued on toward the house. But maybe his steps seemed a little less sure.

"Come on," Abe said from behind him. "He's a stubborn old fool who thinks he knows everything," he said loudly, and the door to the house slammed shut, adding punctuation.

"Are you all right?" Lachlan asked, turning back to Abe. "He hit you hard."

"Not really. It was loud, but not strong." Still, Abe rubbed his cheek.

"Let me see." Lachlan gently lowered Abe's hand. The redness was already fading, but Lachlan figured the sting from his father's rebuke was going to last longer than the pain from the slap. "Does he hit you often?"

"No. But I threw my mother in his face, and that was more than he could stand. I should have known and backed off." Abe sighed. "Yelling at one another doesn't get either of us anywhere. But I wasn't going to let him get away with attacking you for no good reason."

"I don't want to come between you and your dad." Things with Eddie Felder had only gotten started and already there was fallout. It would get truly bad for both him and RaeAnn if Abe's father's reaction was anything to go by.

"You haven't. Things with my dad haven't been good since Mom died." Abe took him by the hand. "Come on. I need to head into town to try to get the parts we think we're going to need, and it's probably best if we make ourselves scarce while he cools down."

He closed the shed door, and Lachlan followed him to the truck. They took off, with Abe spinning the rear tires in his haste to get away. There was definitely a lot of resentment building up on both sides of the relationship between Abe and his dad. Lachlan wished he could help bring them together, but it seemed he only added gasoline to their flame.

Abe flew into town, and Lachlan figured the truck tires actually only touched the road occasionally. At least that was how it felt. Abe clutched the wheel so tightly, his hands were white. "Sometimes my dad makes me want to scream. He's so stubborn and he thinks he knows everything. Mom used to get on him all the time for jumping to conclusions where Randy and I were concerned. Whenever something wasn't done to his satisfaction, he'd start asking questions, but he never wanted an answer. He just wanted to hit us over the head with his way of doing things. Mom was the only one who ever got him to see things a different way." Abe slowed down, and Lachlan took that as a sign that some of the stress was easing. "You were right, though. Whether Dad knows it or not, the reverend has given himself away."

"That may be. But everything we thought is coming true. The reverend is already trying to do damage control, and if your dad is any indication, people are going to believe what the good reverend is spouting." Lachlan trembled, and as they got closer to town, his nerves kicked up more and more. By the time they parked in front of the parts center, he was scared to get out of the truck. "Maybe it's best if I stay here out of sight. I don't want to cause any trouble." People walked by outside, and Lachlan felt as though they were all staring at him.

"Don't…," Abe said. "Everyone is not like my father. At least I hope not." He held out his hand, and Lachlan nodded, squeezing it before releasing it and getting out of the truck. He went inside with Abe and waited while Abe told the man at the counter what he was looking for.

"I'll have to see if I can find the parts you need. It shouldn't be too hard to get. Can you give me a week?"

Lachlan barely heard the words as the other man behind the counter, who had to be about Abe's age, stared at him like he had two heads.

When Abe saw what was going on, he said, "Chuck, this is Lachlan."

"I know who he is." Chuck came around the counter, and Lachlan tensed. "Is it true what they're saying? That someone has come forward about Eddie? It's all over town that you supposedly saw what happened."

"I did," Lachlan said as firmly as he dared, steeling himself for the rebuke. "I don't know what exactly people are saying, but I know what I saw." His nerves getting the best of him, he turned to get the hell out of there.

"Eddie Felder is a bully," Chuck said to his back, and Lachlan whirled around. "He was when we were in school, and I still have the imprints on my back from where he shoved me into lockers. So if he did hurt someone and you saw it, then stick to your guns. There are plenty of people who know what Eddie is like and how his father covers up for him."

Lachlan could barely believe his ears. "Did the reverend do something to you?"

Chuck nodded. "When I finally got up enough nerve to tell someone at school how Eddie had terrorized me, they called in the reverend and he turned everything on me. They listened to him and recommended that I talk to a counselor. My parents were furious, but old man Felder has everyone wrapped around his finger and no one will go against him. But maybe they've gone too far this time." Chuck shook his hand. "Just stand firm and tall."

"I will. I know I'm right," Lachlan said, and Chuck returned to his station behind the counter as another customer came in. He listened to them talk business as Abe finished up. Lachlan shared a man-wave with Chuck as the two of them left. "Where to now?"

"Back to Foster's. I know you probably have work to do, and I can help."

"I promised Grandma Katie that I'd help her today. She wanted to test out some ice cream recipes for Foster, and I have plenty of studying to do. Finals are this week, and graduation is Memorial Day weekend on Sunday. I don't want to mess anything up and have Michigan State decide to change their mind."

"I CAN'T believe that hypocrite! And he's supposed to be a man of God," Grandma Katie spat when Lachlan told her what had happened as they worked in the kitchen an hour later. "He was preaching last week about the Ten Commandments and leaned pretty hard on bearing false witness. He was laying it on thick, and now he's the one doing the lying."

"I suppose he thinks he can control what people think. He sure had an impact on Abe's dad. Apparently word is all over town." He explained about meeting Chuck at Ravenna Parts.

"That's Armitage for you." Grandma Katie tossed aside the cloth she'd been using to wipe her hands. "Don't you worry. I'll stop by and give him a piece of my mind. Well, not too big a piece. I need to keep what mind I have." She shuffled back to the table. "This old body may not look like much, but I can still kick his ass if need be."

Lachlan tried to be serious but couldn't help chuckling, as hard as he tried not to. "I bet you could. But I don't want to cause any more trouble between Abe and his dad."

Grandma Katie shook her head. "That man has been a crotchety ass since Debra died, and he isn't going to change an ounce."

"Abe said the same thing." Lachlan leaned against the table. "We were going to try to develop some special ice cream recipes for Foster." It was probably best that he get off this topic and onto something productive.

"Yes. So what one first?"

"What fruits do you grow? I know we have strawberries."

"There are peaches and some raspberries. Oh, and black currants. You know, we could do some combinations. Peach is a subtle flavor, but maybe we could add a little lemon to bring it out. And I made some amazing pineapple marmalade last year. We could see how that acts as a flavoring."

"That's a great idea. As I see it, the problem with only adding fruit to the ice cream base is that it doesn't stand up to the dairy and the flavor gets lost. That's why companies use artificial flavors or even extracts." The cooking class he had taken as a sophomore was coming in handy for something.

"Then jam should provide the flavor concentrate. It's also sweet, so we need to think about the amount of sugar we use."

"Okay. Then let's get started." Lachlan grabbed a pad of paper. "We should start with a really good vanilla and a chocolate. They're best sellers, and we need those to be special."

Grandma Katie grinned. "Oh, I know how to do that. We'll make the chocolate a little fudgy, and we'll have Harriet pick up some vanilla beans the next time she's in Grand Rapids. Instead of flavors from a bottle, we'll get ours the direct way. I used to do that for Foster's dad when he was a boy, and he once tried to eat an entire batch at a sitting. He would have gotten sick if I hadn't stopped him."

Lachlan laughed. "Okay. I think six flavors to start with. We can see what Foster thinks."

"About what?" Foster asked as he came in the back door with Abe and Javi.

"Ice cream flavors," Grandma Katie said. "We were thinking a rich vanilla, direct from the beans, and a chocolate fudge." She looked over at him. "And instead of straight strawberry, how about strawberry-lime? And we were thinking a peach-lemon. How about pineapple-orange and then a raspberry–black currant? Those should be interesting enough without going too wild."

"Sounds awesome." Foster grinned. "The pasteurization equipment is nearly installed, and we can start getting some of our own product for you to use in a few days."

"Good," Harriet said, joining the group from the living room. "And I need some milk to make another batch of cheeses to take to market next month."

"It sounds like we're all moving ahead." Foster rubbed his hands together excitedly, then reached to pull Javi closer.

Lachlan turned away to give them privacy, wishing Abe was next to him.

"Lachlan and I have work to do," Grandma Katie said. "So you all need to clear out of the kitchen and let us experiment a little."

"I'll bring up the ice cream freezers," Javi offered, and he grabbed Foster by the hand, dragging him willingly along with him.

"Those two," Harriet said happily. "I hope you weren't in any hurry for them."

"Okay. I'm going out to get back to work," Abe said, and Lachlan followed him outside.

"I'm sorry about things with your dad. I didn't mean to make them worse."

"You did nothing wrong." Abe hugged him tightly, which was just what he needed. "There's a saying that no good deed goes unpunished."

"That's exactly what's happening, but I haven't even done anything yet."

"I know. But you're doing what's right, and I'll deal with my father. It might mean that I have to find another place to live, but I can do that. I need to be on my own anyway, eventually." Abe gathered him close, and Lachlan closed his eyes, his head resting against the warmth of Abe's chest. He could do anything as long as Abe stood by him.

"I have to do this. Eddie needs to be stopped or he'll hurt other people." He blinked through the tears, and Abe held him closer.

"I believe in my heart about what you saw. But is there more to it? Did Eddie actually hurt you while you stayed with him and his father?"

Lachlan had hoped that telling about what he saw would stop everyone from looking deeper. He should have known better. Abe was too observant. "Eddie came in my room at night. More than once...." Lachlan squeezed Abe more tightly. "I didn't give him what he wanted, but he kept coming."

"I'll kill him," Abe growled.

"There's no need. I'm going to testify for RaeAnn, and then Eddie isn't going to be around any longer." That was all he wanted.

"How did you get him to stop?"

"He used to get drunk, and if he couldn't find someone to take care of him, he expected me to. But the night before I caught him with RaeAnn, I was ready for him and kneed him hard in the nuts before he could haul them out. The guy's a real piece of work. I wonder if there isn't something wrong with him." Lachlan clung to Abe. "I want him gone where he can't try to hurt me or anyone else anymore."

Abe rubbed a hand up and down his back. "Does the reverend know what he tried to do? He isn't the most open-minded person when it comes to gay people. He has a pretty Old Testament view of things."

"No. I was trying to stay as invisible as possible. I didn't have any other place to go, and once I stood up for myself, I figured Eddie might leave me alone. I'd say he was a pig, but that would be an insult to swine everywhere."

"You can crack jokes at a time like this?"

"It's one of those 'laugh or cry' moments, and laughing is better than falling to pieces." He didn't want to think about all the crap he'd been through between his mother's death and finding his way here to the farm. It had only been a few weeks, but they were best forgotten if at all possible. "I should go back in there and help Grandma Katie."

"I need to get back to work too. But I was hoping we could have another date night."

"Yeah." Lachlan couldn't keep the smile off his face. "I'd like that. The weather is getting warmer, so…." He kissed Abe, wrapping his arms around his neck, trying to convey exactly what he was hoping the date evening would entail. From the clouded expression in Abe's eyes when he pulled away, his message had been received loud and clear. "I'll see you later." Lachlan went back inside and closed the door, breathing deeply so he didn't embarrass himself. He needed a few minutes for things to go down before he went back into the kitchen to face Grandma Katie, who always seemed to be able to read his mind.

"What flavor did you want to start with?" Grandma Katie asked when he entered the room.

"Which ones do we have the ingredients for? I was hoping we could try the strawberry-lime. That sounds really good. But maybe we should start with a basic recipe so we have a good base, and then we can add the flavors."

"All right." Grandma Katie bent down to open one of the lower cupboards and pulled out a huge recipe box. She set it on the table and began going through it. There had to be a thousand recipe cards in it, and from what Lachlan saw, they were all handwritten, and some were stained and yellowed with age. "Let's try this one and see how it works. It's the one I used when my son was a child."

"Okay." Lachlan took the offered card and read through the recipe. Grandma Katie got the ingredients together, and he started mixing them on the stove. It didn't take long before he had what looked like a really good base.

"How does it taste?" Grandma Katie asked, handing him a spoon.

Lachlan dipped a little and let it cool before tasting. "Rich, and the flavor isn't too overpowering, so it should be a good vehicle for whatever we want to put in it."

"Let's split it in half." She got a lime out of the refrigerator and zested it before juicing it, as Lachlan carefully poured half the mixture into a bowl. Grandma Katie measured the zest and the juice into the bowl before adding some of her strawberry jam. The mixture turned slightly pink, but was nothing like the color of commercial ice cream. "Should we add some color?"

"No. Let's let everything be natural." He tasted the mix. "It needs more strawberry."

Grandma Katie agreed and added some more. They tasted it again and made one final adjustment.

Foster and Javi brought up the freezers from the basement, their lips swollen and Javi most definitely flushed. Lachlan pretended not to notice as he took the freezers to the counter, washed them, got one started, and poured in the flavored mixture.

"What's the rest for?" Foster asked.

"So we can refine the recipe. We don't expect to get it right the first time."

"Hey, Abe," Lachlan called as he came in. "We have the first batch in."

"Awesome." Abe came over, kissed him, and then turned to Foster. "I need to go into town to get some bolts and a few clamps. The ones they sent aren't in the best shape, so I figured we shouldn't ask for trouble."

"I'll go with you," Foster said, kissing Javi goodbye, then hurrying outside with Abe.

"I see you wrote down everything." Javi looked over their recipe so far.

"Yeah." Lachlan went to the machine, watching as it whirred. He added more ice and salt. If they made this a commercial enterprise, they were going to need more equipment, but for testing, what they had would work.

"How is it?"

"Starting to thicken up," Lachlan answered, and Grandma Katie put some plastic containers in the freezer to chill while the ice cream was churning. The others stayed out of the way, clearly interested in what they were doing. "It should be another five minutes or so, I'd think." Lachlan added more ice and a little salt, the motor working and then evening out once again. He was patient, watching through the lid until the freezer ground to a near halt. He unplugged it, and Grandma Katie brought over the containers. They scooped out the finished ice cream and got it right into the freezer.

"How long do we need to wait?" Javi asked.

"I kept some out so we can taste it," Grandma Katie said, putting a bowl on the table and handing out spoons. "Harriet!"

She joined them, and they all took a bite. The base was creamy and smooth, luscious in fact, with incredible silky feel. The lime came through nicely with a slight tingle and then the sweetness of the strawberry.

"It's not bad," Harriet said.

"Yeah," Javi agreed.

"It's good, but it needs a little more strawberry. The lime is good, but the strawberry needs to be a little more prevalent to balance it out."

"Then let's get on with the second batch," Grandma Katie said, and the two of them got to work. The next time, it was indeed better, and after multiple tastings and a near empty bowl, they deemed the recipe amazing.

Lachlan and Grandma Katie worked through a few more possibilities and got the peach-lemon right before calling it a day. He went upstairs to clean up, and when he came back down, dressed in his best clothes to go out, he found Abe standing in the living room holding a small bunch of tulips. He looked amazing and almost shy as he handed Lachlan the blooms.

"My mom planted the bulbs for these years ago. They haven't bloomed the last two years since she passed, but this year they're beautiful."

"Yes, they are." Lachlan took the bouquet into the kitchen, where Grandma Katie handed him a vase with water in it. He put the flowers inside and returned to Abe. "We should go." He leaned in for a kiss, and Abe led him out of the house and out to the truck. Lachlan got in and sat back, letting Abe decide where to go.

They ended up on top of the hill once again, sitting on the tailgate. This time Abe had made a picnic dinner, and they ate in companionable silence. Lachlan knew what was likely to come later, and anticipatory heat settled in his belly as he ate his ham sandwich with a crunch of lettuce.

"Things will be different around here when you go away to school."

"That's months away." Lachlan had spent enough time living day to day that it was now hard for him to look that far ahead. His mother's death had taught him that nothing was forever, no matter how much he may want it, and that included things with Abe. He had to live for the now. It was all he had. Lachlan set his sandwich aside and traced the outline of Abe's slightly stubbled jaw with his fingers. "We don't need to think about things like that now."

"I have to." Abe turned to him. "I'm falling in love with you. I know that. It started when I first saw you at the farm, and then, when you agreed to help RaeAnn, I knew you were the kind of man I was looking for. But you'll be leaving in a few months."

"I could stay." Lachlan's heart soared at what Abe was telling him. "Love is worth staying for."

"No. You can't. You need to get to know the bigger world and have the chances few people from this town get." Abe leaned closer, his lips nearly touching Lachlan's. "You have to go to college and learn the things you need to in order to follow your dreams. I think that's what this place is for."

"I don't understand," Lachlan said.

"Javi told me that he and Foster used to come up here when they first met. He called this Dream Hill because it was what he and Foster did up here. They told each other their dreams."

"Did he say what they were?"

Abe shook his head. "He said that if either of them had told anyone else, then they wouldn't have come true. So think about your dream. Not the small ones that take place in the next week or month, but the ones as big as the sky." Abe waved his hands over his head.

"Before I lost my mom, I dreamed of going to college and becoming an engineer. I want to build and help design things. But after she died, my dream became simpler. I guess I dreamed of having a home and being loved."

"Then you have that." Abe pointed down to the farm. "That place with Harriet, Grandma Katie, Foster, and Javi, it's like love personified. Their crops grow better. Dad says it's because they have better land than we do, but I say it's because they do everything with love and care." Abe snickered. "If you tell Foster and Javi what I'm about to tell you, they'll probably kill me, but last summer, I saw the two of them coming out of the corn field near the house. Foster had a blanket and was all disheveled and had corn leaves in his hair."

"You're making that up." Lachlan chuckled.

"Swear to God." Abe held up his hand. "And danged if we didn't have a bumper crop. Every one of Foster's corn fields drew amazing yields."

"So you're saying corn responds to nookie?" Lachlan cackled like crazy. He couldn't help it.

"Don't laugh. It worked last year." Abe's eyes danced, and Lachlan wasn't sure whether to believe him or not. Abe drew him closer, kissing him, and Lachlan forgot about anything other than the richness of Abe's kiss and the way energy flowed through him from such a gentle touch.

"Maybe we can add some of our own this year," Lachlan whispered, pulling Abe closer. His food was forgotten as Lachlan clung to Abe. He slipped off the tailgate and out of Abe's arms. Inside the cab, he yanked out the thick blanket he'd seen earlier and carried it back to where Abe waited. Lachlan knew the steps they were taking needed to be initiated by him. Abe wouldn't be the one to start anything.

Lachlan climbed into the truck bed and laid out the blanket, then sat and waited. Abe turned around and crawled closer, like a panther stalking its prey, wide-eyed and alert for anything. Lachlan loved that.

He lay back as Abe crawled closer, his heat washing over Lachlan like a wave he couldn't stop and didn't want to anyway. Lachlan raised his head off the blanket, watching as Abe drew near, parting his lips so he was ready when Abe took them hard, possessively, his eyes an intense blue that drew Lachlan to him.

Warmth penetrated his shirt just before Abe tugged it over his head, then tossed it against the side of the bed. Abe caressed his chest, plucking gently at a nipple until Lachlan lightly bit Abe's lip, unable to hold back the sweet ecstasy any longer. "Abe, I want you," he breathed softly when Abe pulled back for a brief second. To emphasize his point, he tugged at the buttons of Abe's shirt, getting them open, and then slid the shirt off.

Nothing compared to the heat of skin-on-skin, chest-to-chest contact, with Abe's arms wrapped tightly around him. This was what he needed, at least to begin with. Abe had worked all his life; he was strong and his muscles powerful. That was a turn-on, and when Abe pushed himself upward, taking a second to look down at him, Lachlan teased at a tight, dusky nipple before taking it between his lips. A moan floated over them, the sweetest music Lachlan had ever heard.

He held Abe around the waist, pushing him upward and back to open his pants before Abe pressed him down onto his back. But that gave him access, and Lachlan made the most of it, sliding his hands down Abe's back and inside his jeans, caressing his smooth, hard buttcheeks.

"You're sneaky," Abe whispered with a smile, sucking Lachlan's ear and nearly stopping his ability to think. God, Abe knew how to use his mouth, and Lachlan hoped he got more.

Abe worked Lachlan's pants open, then pushed them down his hips until his cock sprung free. They worked their clothes off, unconscious of where they landed. The excitement between them was too intense for either to take a second to look. All that mattered was each other and the banquet of masculinity the other presented.

"Do you have stuff with you?" Lachlan asked, his mind clear enough to know they needed to be safe.

"Yes," Abe chuckled. "In the glove compartment, but that seems like a million miles away." He climbed off, and Lachlan smiled as Abe trotted bare-assed to the front of the truck and then returned.

Lachlan took that opportunity to gather the remains of their dinner, toss them into the cooler, and set it aside. It had been a miracle it hadn't fallen off the tailgate in their earlier haste. Then he lay back and ran his hand up his shaft.

"You're wicked," Abe purred as Lachlan slowly stroked himself, gazing into Abe's eyes. A packet sailed through the air and landed on the blanket next to him, but Lachlan barely noticed, especially as Abe climbed back into the truck bed and crawled closer, his gaze not leaving him.

Lachlan gasped as Abe took him deep, sliding his lips over his cock, not stopping until Lachlan was buried in his throat. The wet heat surrounding him stole Lachlan's breath. He threw his head back, mouth open in a silent, breathless cry that would have echoed off the land if he'd have been able to find his voice. Instead his soft gasp was for Abe alone. "Abe, I'm…." He laid his head back down, running his fingers through Abe's hair.

Abe pulled away, and Lachlan's cock slapped back against his belly as he tried to catch his breath. "You're amazingly beautiful." Abe leaned closer, kissing him. "God, I want you so bad. But are you sure you're ready?" Abe stroked his chest. "I won't do anything you aren't ready for, and this is a big step."

"I'm ready." Lachlan had wanted to go all the way with Abe for some time, though he'd be lying if he said he wasn't nervous. But this was Abe, his Abe, and he wouldn't hurt him.

"Okay." Abe reached for what he'd tossed earlier, and Lachlan realized there was also lube of some sort. Abe opened it, slicked his fingers, and then teased Lachlan to within an inch of his life before sliding a single finger inside him. "Is that okay?"

"Yeah," Lachlan gasped softly and then groaned, electricity running up his spine as Abe found a spot inside him that seemed to bring his entire body to life. Abe touched him again and again, stretching him but making it fun and oh so sexy. Abe never took his gaze off him, and the attention was nearly as exciting as the way Abe played his body.

Lachlan groaned when Abe pulled his fingers away. He'd really gotten into it. But then Abe shifted between his legs, holding his ankles, and fumbled between them while Lachlan tried not to fly apart with anticipation. Abe moved closer, pressing to him, and held still.

"It's going to hurt at first, and if you want me to stop, just say so."

"Okay." Lachlan gripped the blanket as Abe slid forward, entering him slowly. "Oh God," Lachlan groaned. Abe stopped, and Lachlan shivered, but not with cold. He was so excited and filled with electricity that staying still just wasn't possible.

Abe slowly pressed farther, sliding more easily until he pressed to Lachlan's butt. Then he stilled, and Lachlan breathed as steadily as possible. "All right?" Abe squeaked.

"Yeah. Full," Lachlan managed, and then Abe moved and he lost the ability to speak again.

"That's what it feels like. Just relax and remember to breathe." Abe stroked him gently, and the excitement that had diminished only a few minutes earlier came roaring back. "You're amazing."

"I am?" Lachlan asked.

"Oh yeah." Abe leaned over him, kissing him hard as he moved his hips just a little, sending jolts of excitement through him like ripples on a pond.

Lachlan wanted this to last forever, but he was so excited and everything was so new and different, he was on the edge in a matter of seconds. He did his best to hold off, but his release peaked and washed over him before he knew exactly what to do to stop it. Lachlan floated for a few seconds, realizing that Abe had stopped. Then, after a moment, Abe shifted again, and the floatiness was back and it seemed to stay for a while.

Lachlan didn't want to move in case the spell that surrounded both of them popped like a soap bubble. He didn't want this to end, not for a second, even when Abe shifted to dispose of the spent condom and held him tight. Lachlan barely remembered Abe coming, he was so far out of it by that time. Nothing in his life had ever prepared him for this kind of complete joy.

"We—" Abe began and stilled, only this time Lachlan felt tension increasing by the second. "Someone's coming."

"An engine?"

"It's revving to take the first part of the hill." Abe hurried away and jumped out of the truck, tossing their clothes back into the bed. Lachlan grabbed his boxers and pulled them on, followed by his pants, while Abe jumped back into the bed and did the same.

Lachlan got his shirt on and was working at his shoes as another truck pulled in next to theirs. He recognized it immediately and groaned. That dirty, chipped black paint with blue splotches from some botched paint job could only be Eddie's. Thankfully he was on the far side, but it wouldn't take him long to figure out what he and Abe had been doing. Lachlan hated that this asshole had been the guy to interrupt what had been a perfect evening up till now.

"What do we have here?" Eddie asked as he got out. "A couple of fags." He grinned, showing yellowing teeth.

"Shut your hole," Abe growled, already on his feet. He jumped out of the truck bed, standing between Eddie and Lachlan. "You're nothing more than a bully who preys on other people."

Eddie chuckled. "Prove it." He turned his gaze to Lachlan, and ice ran up Lachlan's spine. The cold, the hatred was so evident, the very air between them chilled.

"We will," Abe said. "Your daddy can't cover this up for you no matter how much he tries."

"No one will believe you." Eddie stepped forward, pushing Abe, who pushed him back, hard. Eddie took a few steps backward in order to regain his balance, and Abe was right there, closing the gap, getting Eddie farther away from Lachlan.

"Want to bet? There are plenty of people who already do," Lachlan added as he climbed out of the bed, staying behind Abe. "You've pulled too much shit and tried to bully too many people in this town for them not to believe us."

Abe pushed Eddie again and received another shove in response. Eddie reared, fist drawing back. Abe ducked Eddie's punch and delivered one of his own right to the gut. "You aren't as strong as you think you are, and I've wanted a piece of you for years. Either back off and leave, or I'll clean your clock and you can go explain to your father how you lost to a fag. I bet daddy will be real pleased."

Eddie's mouth drew into a sneer, and he charged at Abe, fists flying. Abe sidestepped as best he could, but Eddie slammed Abe against the side of the once-black truck. Abe still managed to deck Eddie a good one and push him off. Abe was strong, there was no doubt about that, but he was also a smart fighter, while Eddie relied on nothing but brute force. Abe pushed him back and kept at it while Eddie fought on until he lost his balance and tumbled to the dirt in a heap.

"Had enough?" Abe spat.

Eddie jumped to his feet, but Abe seemed ready, countering his move, pushing him back once again. There wasn't a great deal of room, and Eddie got close to the side of the hill, then moved forward once again.

"Lachlan, check the truck. I think I saw movement inside." Abe called, and Lachlan hurried around the front of Eddie's truck and then over to the passenger door.

"Keep away from my shit!" Eddie groaned.

Lachlan turned, watching as Abe countered Eddie, pushing him back farther.

"You're the only shit here—well, that and your truck." Abe charged this time, and Eddie couldn't counter. He stepped back out of the way and disappeared from sight. A steady stream of blue rose up the side of the hill, growing fainter but still present.

"Is he okay?" Lachlan asked as he peered over the edge.

"Yes. He's covered in dirt and picking burrs out of his clothes." Abe turned with a smile. "I've wanted to beat the crap out of him for years." He came closer as Lachlan pulled open the door of the truck.

"Oh crap." Abe reached in and felt the neck of the girl passed out and lying across the bench seat. "She's alive."

"The asshole must have drugged her," Abe said from next to him. "That's Carolyn Sommers. She's new in town." He pulled out his phone. "Crap, no signal." He snapped a few pictures for evidence.

"What do we do? We can't leave her here in case Eddie comes back."

"We have to get her some help." Abe turned to him. "This is going to put you and me both in the good reverend's sights even more than we are now."

Lachlan stood tall. "So what? We need to help her."

Abe nodded slowly. "Yes, we do."

CHAPTER 8

ABE REACHED into the truck and gently gathered Carolyn into his arms. He picked up her dead weight, grateful she was a little slip of a thing, and carefully carried her to his truck. "Gather up all of our things as fast as you can, and we'll take her to the hospital." Abe got her settled, and by the time he was done, Lachlan had the blanket and picnic things cleared away and the truck bed buttoned up. He got in and held Carolyn so she didn't flop over while Abe started the engine and began the descent down the hill.

He went as fast as he dared, expecting to encounter Eddie along the way, but he made it to the bottom before he saw Eddie trudging through the mud, heading his way, limping a little. Not that he intended to stop to help him. Abe didn't look back as he made the turn toward the main road and then headed to town.

"Carolyn, are you okay? Can you talk to me?" Lachlan asked her gently over and over.

She groaned and started to move before putting her hand over her mouth. Abe pulled to a stop and helped her out of the truck, where she threw up by the side of the road.

"Do you feel better?" Lachlan asked, handing her a napkin as she straightened.

"Yeah. But everything is still spinning. What happened?" She leaned over and threw up once again before wiping her mouth. Lachlan put his arm around her to help her into the truck. "What's wrong with me?" She sat back in the seat, and Abe got into the truck, avoiding the mess, and continued the drive to town.

"What do you remember?" Lachlan asked gently.

"I...." She put her hands on the sides of her head. "I was working at the Piggly Wiggly. I'm the assistant manager. I just started there a few weeks ago. This guy came in every day. He was nice and he smiled at me, and yesterday he asked if I had a day off." She leaned back and shut her eyes. "He was charming in a cute sort of way and asked me out. I told him I had to work until five, and he said he'd pick me up. We went to a drive-through and got burgers and drinks. Afterward I had to go to the bathroom, so he stopped for me. Everything is fuzzy after that."

Abe continued driving but gripped the wheel tighter. This whole scenario was becoming very familiar. "Did he say what his name was?"

"Eddie. He said his dad was a minister in town." She groaned, keeping her eyes closed.

Lachlan leaned forward and caught his eye. Abe wasn't sure what to say or how much to tell her of what they suspected. "Do you remember anything else?" Lachlan asked.

"Just waking up in this truck. I must have fallen asleep. I didn't have anything to drink, so…." She put her hands over her face. "Oh God, did he do something to me?"

"We're taking you to the hospital so you can find out," Abe said. "We aren't going to hurt you, and we'll be there as soon as we can." He drove quickly, thankful for no traffic, and pulled into the hospital emergency entrance. "Lachlan will take you in while I park." Lachlan opened the door and helped Carolyn get out. As soon as the door closed, Abe pulled out and drove to the lot, parked, and hurried back inside. Lachlan and Carolyn weren't in the waiting area, so he asked about them at the desk.

"They're in the back. Please have a seat, and I'll have someone come talk to you," the lady behind the desk said, and Abe sat down.

The people who came to speak to him were police officers, who showed up ten minutes later. Abe told them everything that happened, including the details of the fight and how Lachlan found Carolyn.

"She isn't the only person. Lachlan saw him assault someone else and she's pressing charges—at least, that's what I understand." Abe answered all the questions he could and gave them his contact information.

Lachlan came out and escorted him back. "Carolyn wants to talk to you," he explained, and once he entered the small cubicle where they had her, Lachlan sat in the chair next to the bed and Carolyn took his hand.

"I wanted to thank both of you. I don't know what would have happened if you hadn't been there." She sniffed. "They took blood samples, and the police asked if I'd been sick."

"I explained the location, and I guess they're on their way to take samples to prove that she was drugged," Lachlan said softly, still holding her hand.

"He's done this before?" Carolyn asked.

Abe nodded in confirmation. "Yes. He's a predator." He turned as an officer came in. The room was pretty crowded, so Abe excused himself to give them more room. He stepped back out into the waiting room, where Lachlan joined him fifteen or so minutes later.

"Is she all right?"

"Yes. They had her call her parents and they're driving in. One of the officers is going to stay with her. They said they want to talk to me tomorrow, and I gave them the address of the farm." Lachlan shook a little. "I have no idea how someone could be like this."

"There's something wrong with him. It's the only explanation. But Eddie isn't going to get away with it this time. There's too much evidence, and his father can't do a thing to protect him now." Abe stood and took Lachlan's hand. "Come on. Can we go home?"

"Yes. I made sure it was okay with the police." Lachlan leaned closer and looked up at him. "One thing is for sure. You and I have the most interesting dates." They both laughed, but it was tinged with regret.

"How about we try to keep them more normal in the future?" Abe grinned. He could use a little normal quietness for the next few months. He wanted to spend as much time with Lachlan as possible. They only had so much time before Lachlan went to school, and then doubt set in as to how a relationship between them could possibly last through the separation and the changes they were sure to experience over the next four years. He wanted a happy summer. That's all he could ask for.

"Let's go on home. I don't think there's anything else we can do tonight." Lachlan yawned, and Abe checked his watch. In the time between the confrontation with Eddie, getting Carolyn to the hospital, and now leaving, night had fallen and it was well after ten. Harriet and Grandma Katie would be worried if they didn't get home soon. Lachlan got in the truck and called the farm to let them know he was on his way back. "I'm fine. But Eddie has been up to his tricks." He continued talking while Abe drove and finished up about the time he pulled into the farm drive.

"Are you going to be okay?" Abe asked.

"Yes. I'm fine, but I wasn't the one taking on Eddie."

Abe pulled to a stop, and Lachlan slid across to him as soon as he stopped the engine. "Did he punch you?" Lachlan checked over his hands and then his head. Abe figured his shirt and pants were the next to go.

"I'm okay, really." Abe held Lachlan, and they sat for a while, just being quiet, as the windows fogged over. "He isn't a good fighter, and the only time he got anything on me was when he slammed me into the truck." Abe touched Lachlan's chin, tilting his head upward. "You should go inside, and I need to go home so my father and I can do our best to pretend the other one doesn't exist." He kissed him, enjoying a final taste of his sweet lips before releasing Lachlan so he could get out. "I'll see you tomorrow." Abe waited for Lachlan to go inside before driving home.

The house was quiet, with a single light burning in the living room. Abe figured his father was in bed, so he was surprised to find the television on low and his father sitting in his chair.

"We need to talk," his dad said in an ominous tone.

Abe sighed. "What is it, Dad? I've had a tough day."

"Were you out with that Lachlan kid? You know he's trouble."

Abe shook his head and rolled his eyes. "You don't know anything." He walked closer until he stood over his father. "We had a picnic on the hill, and Eddie came up there. He mustn't have seen us.

He started calling us names, and he and I fought." Abe automatically brushed off his shirt.

"I raised you better than that."

"And if someone had threatened Mom, you would have stood by? Come on, Dad, you'd have beat the crap out of them. I stood up to Eddie. He had it coming." Abe smiled. "Anyway, he fell down the side of the hill because he's such a dumbass. He had a girl in his truck that he'd drugged. He was bringing her up there to assault her. She's at the hospital now, and her family is on the way." He put his hands on his hips and narrowed his gaze. "So are you willing to call Lachlan a liar now?"

His father looked up at him like his entire world had been shaken.

"It's the truth, Dad. We spent the last few hours in the emergency room making sure Carolyn was okay."

"Carolyn Sommers?" his father asked softly, and Abe nodded. "I see her at the store all the time. She's helped me at Piggly Wiggly and was interested in carrying our eggs if we could get enough production."

"You know she's new in town, and Eddie tried to take advantage of her."

"I really hope she's okay," his father muttered. "And you really think Eddie... would do that?" His father shook his head.

"They're running tests at the hospital and the police are involved. They're taking it seriously, and they will with RaeAnn as well now that there are two women making complaints. The reverend can't hide from this, and he's going to have to answer a lot of questions about how much he knew of his son's activities."

"That...." His father paused. "God, what are we all going to do?"

"Try standing behind the victims and giving them the support they need so they aren't hurt again and again. People are usually afraid to come forward because they won't be believed. You did your part in that. Now, what are you going to do to help that stop?" Abe eased his stance, dropping his arms to his side. "There are likely to be more girls, some who you've known for years, who could come forward. Eddie is a sexual predator."

"I had no idea."

"I know you didn't, and you were being loyal to a man you thought was worthy of your loyalty. But he's covered up for Eddie at least once, and the good reverend needs to face the consequences."

His father nodded slowly. "I'm going to call the members of the council at the church and tell them what's going on. We need to take action to make sure our families and children are safe." He sighed. "And you and your friend were the ones to bring this to light?"

Abe nodded. "It was Lachlan who was willing to go out on a limb and back up RaeAnn, even though he knew people weren't likely to believe him." He gave his dad his best version of the evil eye. "What did you want to talk to me about?"

His father seemed far away all of a sudden. "You know that the farm hasn't been doing so well."

"Yes. Randy and I talked about it, and he's going to try some things."

"I want you to come and work here, with your brother and me, until we can get back on our feet."

Abe should have seen this coming. "How much are you going to pay me? Foster pays me a salary for the work I do, and I'm self-sufficient except for the fact that I have a room in the house. I rarely eat here, and I've given you money as room and board every month to help out."

"This is your home and we're your family." His father seemed hurt.

"It hasn't felt much like a home since Mom died, and I have a job and a chance to start making a life of my own. It's what kids do when they grow up." He sighed softly, wondering how to say what he wanted to say. "You made it very clear that you wanted the farm to stay in one piece, so you decided to pass it on to Randy because he's the oldest. I can't say I agree with your decision 100 percent, but it makes a kind of sense. Randy's future is here, and you need to work with him to make the farm prosperous again. But that isn't going to come with your old-fashioned ways and ideas. You need to think of the farm as a business the way Foster does."

"But—"

"Dad, I'd be just a slave here, and I won't be that to a farm that I'm not going to see anything out of. You made your decision, and I'm making mine." Abe turned and went right up the stairs to his bedroom, though he didn't think he was going to sleep very well.

IN THE morning, things between him and his father were back to their usual frostiness. His father sat across from him at the breakfast table, staring down at his plate of eggs and sausage without saying a word or even looking at him. Abe didn't think his father was being reasonable about anything, but he wasn't going to back down. He'd worked hard to obtain his measure of independence. His dad finished eating and Abe put his dishes in the sink before saying goodbye and going to work.

He followed the same routine all week, with his dad barely saying anything to him and Abe doing his best to get on with things. After all, when he wasn't at home, he was generally at the farm, and in the afternoons, Lachlan was there when he got home from school.

"It's Sunday, and I see you're dressed to go to church." It was the most his dad had said to him the entire week. He was already dressed and ready to go.

"No. Today is graduation, and I'm going into town to the ceremony this afternoon." Abe undid his tie and tried tying it again, standing in front of the mirror in the bathroom. He finally got it so it looked right. "I'm not setting foot in any church presided over by Reverend Hypocrite and you know it."

"I think you should go. Church is important. You can go to the graduation afterwards." His dad sounded as though he were making a pronouncement from the pulpit.

"I could but I won't, Dad. I'll decide what's important in my life, and I'm not setting foot there. I already told you. I'm going to Lachlan's graduation. We all are."

"We all?"

"Yeah."

"Morning, Dad," Randy said, coming up the stairs. "The herd's milked and the morning chores are done. I'm going with Abe. We'll see you later."

Abe did his best not to look at his dad, but couldn't help it. His face was beet red, and there might have been smoke coming out his ears, he was so angry. Abe might have chuckled, but the hurt and confusion in his dad's eyes stopped him. He really didn't understand what was happening at all.

"Lachlan is Abe's boyfriend and he doesn't know a lot of people here in town, so I thought it would be nice if I went along to help support him. You know all about the scandal with the reverend and Eddie, and Lachlan has taken more than his share of grief over it." Randy patted his dad on the shoulder. "He's really a nice guy."

"Oh...." His dad turned, walked down the steps, and soon after, the back door closed.

"Everything has knocked the legs out from under him. The troubles with the farm, this with the reverend, and you suddenly having a boyfriend," Randy said. "Everything he relied on and used as a rock to build his life on doesn't seem quite so solid any longer."

"I suppose not," Abe said, sighing. "But I don't know how to help him. I want to make him understand, but he won't even try." He went to his room to get his jacket and checked the time.

"Dad's just like the rest of us—stubborn as hell," Randy said from the hall. "Come on. We need to get to town and find a parking place, and you don't want to arrive late."

"Foster and Javi said they'd save us places. Apparently they're all going." He grabbed his wallet and keys from the scarred top of the dresser. The piece of furniture had seen a lot of hard use. Now that he was ready, he and Randy went down the stairs and out to Abe's truck for the drive into town.

Randy easily found a parking spot, and they walked around to the central courtyard of the school. A stage had been set up at one end, with places for the band next to it, and chairs were spread out on the lawn in sections for the graduates, as well as the audience. Thankfully the day was sunny and warm. If the weather threatened, they'd move the ceremony into the gym, but it was so much nicer outside.

Foster, Javi, Grandma Katie, and Harriet had saved them seats near the front, and the six of them sat together as others filed in.

Grandma Katie sat next to him, turning as she grinned like a cat who ate the canary. "Lachlan got an unexpected graduation present today." Abe thought she was going to burst into song, she was so excited.

"What kind of present?" Abe couldn't help smiling.

"I went to church this morning and Reverend Felder stood up in front of the congregation and announced that he was going to be moving on. It took all my self-control not to stand up and clap." She dang near giggled, and Harriet glared at her for two seconds before smiling as well. Clearly she was just as pleased.

"Did he say anything more?" Abe wanted to cheer at the great news.

"He tried to make it sound as though he'd gotten a calling somewhere else, but word is all around town now and I don't think anyone is buying it. Of course, everyone was talking about it after church. My only disappointment is not being able to stay to hear what was being said."

"Gossiping isn't nice," Harriet commented gently.

Grandma Katie rolled her eyes and leaned closer. "If you can't say something nice, come sit by me."

Abe nearly lost it, and Randy stifled a snort next to him. Regardless of how it came out, this was at least some good news and well past time for it.

The chairs filled as the band tuned their instruments and took their places. When the band began "Pomp and Circumstance," everyone turned as the first graduates entered in their blue gowns with white accents. It took him a few seconds before he found Lachlan, and Abe smiled, knowing the second Lachlan saw him and receiving a smile in return. Once everyone was seated, the speeches began, but Abe paid little mind, his attention on Lachlan, locked on his gaze across the small sea of people. He knew today would be hard for him, and Abe hoped Lachlan knew there were people in the audience who cared for him very much, even if his mother wasn't there.

Various dignitaries got up to speak, and then the class speaker—a blonde girl, tall, thin, and striking—approached the podium. "Today we move on in our lives. This is a transition. We leave behind the rigors and security of high school and take our first steps out into the wide world." She went on after that, but Abe barely listened, looking over at Lachlan, knowing what she had just said was true. All of them, including Lachlan, were moving on, out into the wider world, and cold, steely fear raced up his spine. That transition was what Lachlan needed—Abe knew that. But hearing the speaker say it brought to mind just how hard it was going to be to say goodbye at the end of the summer, and how unlikely it was that Lachlan would choose to find his way back to Abe once he had experienced what the world had to offer him.

CHAPTER 9

SHERRY BEGAN her speech. "Today we move on in our lives. This is a transition. We leave behind the rigors and security of high school and take our first steps out into the wide world." Lachlan knew she was trying to be uplifting and joyous. She wore her usual perky smile, and her energy bubbled off the stage to enthrall the crowd. She was a great speaker, and Lachlan had known she'd be the one chosen to give the address. Sherry really deserved it.

But none of her positivity seemed to get through to him. Instead, those words invoked fear and little else. He knew he should be happy to be finishing school and to be able to get away from this town and all the mess involving Eddie and his father. But he wasn't. The brouhaha with the reverend and his son would be over soon enough. It seemed that public opinion was turning away from Reverend Felder by the minute.

What bothered him was leaving the farm, and more importantly, Abe. He had found someone to help him start to heal his battered and bruised heart and soul. Actually, everyone at the farm had aided him with that. Harriet listened to him and even came into his room before going to bed just to make sure he was all right. A few times he hadn't been, and she'd sat up with him for hours, talking and holding his hand while he poured out the longing to have his mother back. Grandma Katie was a balm for the soul. Her humor and no-nonsense attitude were just what he needed, and he could always count on her to tell him exactly how things were in a way that was never hurtful and usually made him smile. He loved her like the grandmother he never had and always wanted.

Foster and Javi were the brothers he'd always dreamed of. They loved each other, and that love acted like a beacon, showing Lachlan

143

what he wanted as well. They included him and helped him, even teased and picked on him sometimes, especially whenever he tried to milk one of the cows. He always fumbled because he was afraid the large beasts would sit on him. Maybe his gay genes gave him an aversion to udders? Whatever it was, domesticated ungulates were definitely not his thing.

Then, of course, there was Abe, who had become a part of his heart. The owner of it. Lachlan wasn't sure if he'd given it or if Abe had stolen it, but it didn't matter. A piece of him belonged to Abe, and he was scared to death of leaving. Abe was an incredible man, and with Lachlan gone at school for months at a time… how was that going to work? Worse, what if Abe met someone he liked more than Lachlan? Would he be able to survive it? And as much as he loved and treasured all the people at the farm, who he thought of as family, once he'd gone away, would they still feel the same way? He had no real right to expect that they would. He was just a kid they'd helped off the street, literally. His ties to them were only a few months old, not built on years of trust and hard work, like a real family.

Lachlan needed to get all the thoughts racing through his head out of it or else he wasn't going to be able to contain them and his brain would explode out of his ears, covering the girls on either side with what little gray matter he possessed. His mother would have told him that he was overthinking things and to try to relax, take it one day at a time, and enjoy what he had while he had it.

Hearing his mother's voice in his head brought tears to his eyes, and he nearly missed the point where they stood and headed up for the diplomas to be handed out. After the last one had returned to their seats, the graduates all stood, cheered, and waved their hats in the air. Apparently they were not to be thrown in case someone got hurt. He and the rest of the graduates then filed out and waited in the back, where they would be joined by their friends and family. The collective happiness around him was nearly overwhelming, especially since he felt almost none of it. Thinking of his mother had sent what excitement he had flying away like dust in a tornado.

"I know this was hard," Abe whispered, and just like that Lachlan was engulfed in strong, sure arms and held tightly. He buried his face in Abe's shirt, hoping everyone else didn't see him coming apart while they were celebrating around him.

"How...?"

"I saw all of it on your face—the fear, the pain, all written plain as day to anyone who watches and knows you." Abe turned slightly, helping move Lachlan away from the others. "Give yourself a few minutes and then we'll get out of here."

"I don't want to be a baby," Lachlan whispered, pulling back slightly, hoping he wasn't making a spectacle of himself.

"Lachlan."

He knew that voice and looked up from Abe's shirt into the eyes of Sherry, the girl who had given the speech that had reduced him to a blubbering idiot.

"I saw you while I was speaking." She smiled sadly.

"You made me think of my mom." He wiped his eyes, and Abe pulled a tissue out of his pocket. Lachlan took it gratefully and wiped his nose, thankful to Abe for being so thoughtful.

"I understand. It was hard for me not to think of my dad while I was speaking."

Lachlan nodded, remembering that her father had died in a farming accident last year.

"He would have wanted to be here more than anything, and he told me I needed to work and study hard so I would have choices in my life. And I like to think that he is here, watching over me, and I bet your mom is too."

Lachlan nodded feebly as Harriet and Grandma Katie cut a path through the milling crowd in an effort to get to him. Once they arrived, Grandma Katie stood on the other side of Abe, an arm gently around his waist. "She is here. I know you're right." Suddenly, Lachlan could feel her presence in Grandma Katie's concern and Harriet's proud expression. Foster and Javi seemed excited and bouncy as well. "You gave a great talk. Best one of the day."

145

"Thanks." She rushed forward, hugging him quickly, and then moved away.

Others greeted him, and Lachlan put on a happy face and tried his best to get into the spirit of the day. As the number of graduates and their families began to thin, Abe guided their entire group out of the courtyard to where they'd all parked.

"Are we going back to the farm?" Lachlan asked. He wanted to change out of this getup and maybe work in the garden. He needed to do something normal and mind-numbing, preferably alone. What should have been a celebration of achievement only seemed to highlight what he didn't have and what he truly wished he still had in his life.

"Yes. Randy's going to ride with us," Harriet told him.

Lachlan climbed into the truck with Abe, still holding his diploma, and sat back, wondering what he was going to do for the summer. Foster had already told him that there was plenty of work to do at the farm and that he would pay him so he could start saving up for college.

"I know this is really hard," Abe said.

"I thought I was over it, you know. That maybe enough had happened...."

"Nope. There will always be things that remind you of her. It's just how things are. You get to recognize it, and yet there are times when it will take you completely by surprise." Abe smiled a bit sadly. "I was thinking some of my mother today too."

Abe continued driving, but Lachlan paid no attention. All he wanted was for the pain to be over. He'd lost his only parent, and what ached more than the initial pain of loss was the lingering reminder of how alone he truly was, over and over again. His mother wasn't coming back, and no matter how much he wished it weren't true and that this whole ordeal was some huge joke, it was reality, and he kept thinking that the sooner he accepted it and moved on, the easier things would get.

"Where are you?" Abe asked gently.

"At the cemetery where I buried my mother. Can we go there? It's the one on the west side of town. I really want to tell her some things."

Abe turned his attention to the car just ahead of them, the one Foster was driving, and bit his lower lip. "Yes. We can go, but how about we do that a little later?"

"Sure. I should have asked when we weren't headed the other way." He slumped on the seat and closed his eyes, trying to find some sort of happy place. Nothing was working.

Abe pulled into the farm drive, lined with almost a dozen cars. "What's going on?"

Abe pulled to a stop. "Did you really think Harriet and Grandma Katie would let something like today go by without doing something for you?" He turned off the engine. "We weren't sure what your mom might have had in mind, and none of us is trying to take her place, but we wanted to throw you a little party." Abe opened his door and looked at him over his shoulder. "If you need a few minutes, take what you need and come on in."

Lachlan panned his gaze at the largely strange cars and trucks, wondering who was waiting for him inside. He opened his door, figuring he might as well get it over with. He followed Abe inside and was greeted with a small group of smiles.

RaeAnn had come, and so had Carolyn, both smiling and giving him a hug, each whispering their thanks for standing up for them.

Abe's brother, Randy, shoulder-bumped him as he carried a tray of food into the dining room. "If my brother gives you grief, you come to me and I'll tell you all kinds of stories he doesn't want anyone to know." Randy hurried away, probably making sure he was out of range.

Lachlan recognized a few people from the church and some of the people from the bank where his mother had worked. They all told him how much they'd liked his mother.

"Lachlan," Mr. Garvan, his mother's former boss, said before taking him aside. "Every year the bank offers a small set of scholarships to employees and their children. We've done it for the past ten years, and this year, everyone on the committee—most of them worked with your mother at one time or another—decided that this year and for the next three years, we'd offer a single scholarship." He handed Lachlan an envelope.

"But, sir, I didn't apply...."

"Your mother did for you. She was very proud of how hard you'd worked and how well you did in school. She always said you would be the one to watch." He shook Lachlan's hand. "If there's anything you need, come see me, and I'll be available to try to offer any advice that I can."

"Thank you." Lachlan clutched the envelope and was almost afraid to open it. He jumped a little when Abe's arm encircled his waist, then relaxed into the touch. He needed that closeness right now.

Mr. Garvan nodded and fell into conversation with a few other people from the bank, which gave Lachlan a chance to breathe and get his thoughts together.

His mother truly was here; it seemed she was never very far away.

"Do you want me to put that on the table with the other gifts?"

"Others?" Lachlan asked quietly. "There are others?"

"Of course." Abe rolled his eyes at him, and Lachlan let him take the envelope and set it on the table near the door, where a few wrapped gifts and some envelopes lay in a jumbled pile.

He sniffled and pulled the tissue from earlier out of his pocket, wiped his nose, and shoved it away again. He smiled up at Abe, letting him guide him around the room so he could talk to everyone.

"The food is ready," Grandma Katie said, and everyone gravitated into the dining room, where a buffet of near epic proportions had been set out. Why they thought so much food was needed was beyond him, but it looked amazing.

"Katie, your cookies are always the best in the county," Mr. Garvan said, covering his mouth as he spoke.

Carolyn stood next to him, and Lachlan shared a shy smile with her. "I'm glad you came."

"How could I not? You and Abe here did an amazing thing for me." She leaned a little closer. "Can I speak with you a minute? I don't want to ruin the party and all, but there are some things you deserve to know." Her tone was ominous and Lachlan nodded slowly. He didn't like the sound of that at all.

"Sweetheart, are you having a good time?" Grandma Katie asked as she came over, and Lachlan pasted a smile on his face. Whatever was happening would wait until he talked with her. She was more important than most anything else.

"Yes, I really am." He hugged her more tightly than he intended, but his nerves were running nearly out of control. "Thank you for everything."

"It was nothing really." She was obviously trying to underplay what she'd done.

"No. It was everything." He released her, and Harriet called Katie over.

Lachlan caught Carolyn's gaze. Thankfully Abe was right next to him, and they stepped outside into the sunshine that didn't seem so bright at the moment.

"I'm sorry to interrupt the party and all, but the police called this morning and told me that they issued a warrant for Eddie."

"Why do I get the idea that isn't good news?" Lachlan gripped Abe's hand.

"They can't find the little bastard and think he skipped town. They put a call out for the entire state. I should have known the shit would try to run. The snake." Hurt colored her voice, which was also touched with fear.

Lachlan gasped. He should have known a guy as cowardly and sneaky as Eddie Felder would try to get away rather than taking the heat for what he'd done. Still Lachlan hadn't been prepared for it.

"Yeah. He always thought the rules didn't apply to him," Abe interjected with a huff. "Cowardly little shit." Abe touched his back gently and some of the tension drained away. "Are you living alone?"

She shook her head. "I moved in with a friend until he's back in custody. As soon as they told me, I found myself looking out the window all the time, half expecting to see him outside. The police also suggested I'd be safer not living alone. If he were smart, he'd have already left the state, but I don't think he is, and it wouldn't surprise me if he's still in town." Abe opened the door and they stepped inside, still talking.

"Why do you think so?" Lachlan took a piece of Harriet's homemade cheese from a plate on the kitchen table without thinking. It was creamy smooth as it slid down his throat, but he barely tasted it. He got a small glass of punch in a paper cup and drank it down, the cold soothing away the slight ache from his earlier crying. He took a second to try to let go of this Eddie crap and concentrate on the special day that everyone had so generously worked to give him.

"Eddie isn't the type to let anything go," Abe said when Carolyn hesitated. "In school, any slight had to be followed up, any insult returned fast and furious. I mean, he must justify his behavior in his own mind somehow, so that means the people who stopped him are in the wrong and he would want to even the score."

Lachlan turned to RaeAnn, who stood near Grandma Katie, talking quietly, and he wondered if she had someone to stay with.

"Us girls stick together," Carolyn said, most likely following his gaze. "She told me she's moved back in with her brother for a while."

"All this drama and fear because one guy couldn't keep his hands, and other parts, away from where they didn't belong." Eddie made him angry, and Lachlan crushed the cup in his hand as he automatically made a fist.

"Let's talk about something happier." Carolyn leaned forward and hugged him gently. "Today is a big day for you. Where are you going to school?"

"Michigan State. I'm going to be an engineer. It's what I always wanted to do." He hadn't figured out exactly what sort yet, but that would come. Recently he thought he wanted to have something to do with animals or maybe food processing. The farm had opened his eyes to a whole new world of possibilities.

"Lachlan is going to do amazing things," Abe said, and Lachlan turned as RaeAnn approached. She said hello quietly, and Lachlan hugged her gently. Then she and Carolyn drifted away. "They need to talk," Abe said.

"I'm really surprised more people haven't come forward," Lachlan mused as he watched them before heading back to the buffet table.

Abe looked sheepish. "I'm sorry. I should have told you. I heard that two other women have been in contact with the police. They aren't saying their names yet, but there were more, as we suspected."

This was one time when Lachlan hated being right.

"Come on, you two," Javi said as he hurried over. "You need to eat, and then Lachlan can open his presents." As excited as Javi was, the presents could have been for him too.

Lachlan took a plate and got some food, with Abe doing the same. Then they sat in the living room and talked to everyone. The energy in the house seemed so positive, and slowly some of the longing and emptiness he'd felt earlier dissipated somewhat. It didn't go away, but it wasn't nearly as strong.

Once everyone had eaten, Harriet came into the room with a chocolate cake, the scent filling the space, making Lachlan's full stomach rumble at all the chocolaty goodness. "Sweetheart, you need to cut the first piece." Harriet handed him the knife, and he did his best to take out a piece without doing too much damage. Everyone clapped, and Lachlan smiled. He took the first bite, as Harriet instructed, because she believed it good luck, and then she set about serving everyone else.

"Have you given any thought to long-term plans?" one of the ladies from the church asked. He remembered her for her sweet, grandmotherly nature, but not her name.

"Esther, Lachlan is going to Michigan State on full scholarship," Harriet told her. "And when he has breaks, he's going to come back here. This is his home for as long as he wants it."

Lachlan's throat tightened, and he took another bite of cake to try to cover for the fact that he was about to break into tears once again.

"He isn't your kin," Esther said without heat or malice, more of a statement of fact.

"We are all each other's kin," Harriet said with a mirrored tone. "Grandma Katie and I talked it over, and we decided to adopt him into our family. He'll be the first one to graduate college." She smiled, and Esther filtered away. "Old gossipy biddy," Harriet muttered. "She and Katie have known each other for years, and if you want the entire town to know something, just tell her. She's faster than the internet."

"Harriet, you don't need to put yourself and your family out on my account. You've all been so nice, and—"

"Nonsense. You're family now, and we meant it." Harriet looked to where Esther was talking to Grandma Katie. "Do you want to be the one to argue with her?" Harriet patted his shoulder. "We love having you here." To his surprise, she kissed him on the cheek, then left him and Abe alone.

"You should open your gifts so you can thank everyone before they leave," Abe reminded him, and Lachlan went to where the presents waited and picked the first one. It was quite large, from Javi and Foster, and inside was a sturdy backpack for his books. He lifted it out and gaped at the iPad underneath. It was too much. He looked around, unsure if this was actually for him.

"You're going to need it for school," Javi said, bounding over. "Foster got me one for Christmas, and I love mine. If you need help, I can show you how to get it set up."

"Thank you." He hugged Javi and Foster as well before opening the next gift. The card said it was from Harriet and Grandma Katie.

"Something to put in that fancy bag the boys gave you," Grandma Katie said with a smile as Lachlan unwrapped a MacBook. "You'll need one for your work, and Javi said you could link it to the iPad so you'd always have access to everything." She shrugged and waved a hand at him. "I have no idea how all that works, but I hope you love it."

Lachlan threw his arms around her neck, completely overwhelmed. He had a hard time wrapping his mind around how kind they were to him.

Grandma Katie patted his back, then pulled away, looking thoughtful. "Now don't go getting all gooey and thinking this is too much." Leave it to her to read his mind. "It's required for school, and now you can go in the fall and be as ready as everyone else." She squeezed him and slowly stepped back.

"But how can you all spend this much on me?"

"Please. It wasn't that much." She moved away so Harriet could take her place, and Lachlan was seconds from crying once again.

Eventually he was able to open the other gifts. Most of them were cards with a little money. Lachlan was simply grateful they remembered him. He thanked everyone, then went upstairs to change into more comfy clothes. When he returned, the party was winding down. A few people remained, talking with Harriet and Grandma Katie. Javi and Foster were most likely out with the herd, and Lachlan left the house, heading to the garden. A few plants had sprouted, and he checked them over, pulling any weeds that tried to get a start. Mostly he needed something to do that allowed him to clear his head.

"I thought I'd find you here," Abe said from the edge of the huge garden space.

"I needed to think." Lachlan got the last of the weeds and stood, stretching his back. "I can't believe they did all this for me."

Abe waited for him and took his hand. "I have my present to give you." He led Lachlan to his truck, and they got inside. "Don't worry. I told Harriet and Grandma Katie that we'd be gone for a little while."

Lachlan got inside and wasn't at all surprised when Abe drove toward the hill and ascended the steep incline to the top. He pulled to a stop at the spot with the best view and lowered the windows. "I wasn't sure exactly what I should get you, but I knew I wanted something special." Abe fidgeted on the seat and then leaned over to open the glove box. He pulled out a small, long box wrapped in light blue paper. "If you don't like it, it's okay. But I wanted to get you something so you'd always remember me."

"You didn't have to," Lachlan said even as he tore excitedly into the paper. He opened the box, which held a gold chain with a small round gold medallion with a rearing horse etched on it.

"I wanted you to remember our first date, and if you do, then you won't forget me."

Lachlan lifted the chain out of the box and carefully put it around his neck. "It's wonderful, thank you." He turned to Abe. "But what I don't understand is how you think I'll forget you. How could I? You came along and helped me get my legs under me again when I didn't think that was even possible." Didn't Abe realize how amazing he was and that anyone would be a fool to let him go?

Abe didn't move or turn, just stared out the window.

"You need to talk to me." Lachlan's voice broke, and he swore at himself. He was not a baby, and yet his body was acting as though he were.

Abe did turn to him then, the blank look replaced with a gentle smile. "You're right, and this is a huge day. We should be celebrating. Not only are you legally an adult, but you've graduated from high school with an amazing future ahead of you."

"If that's so, then why do you sound like you're being led on a forced march or something?" Lachlan asked. "I know forced happiness when I hear it." He'd been the king of it for weeks so everyone around him wouldn't worry that he was as close to falling apart as he seemed to feel all the time.

"It's nothing, really. I'm always looking for trouble even when there isn't any."

Lachlan didn't completely believe him.

"So, do you like your gift? Is it okay?"

"It's gorgeous," Lachlan said with a grin, touching the medallion at the base of his throat. The sun was still rather high in the sky, shining brightly, bathing everything below in light. "I can't believe everyone did all that for me." In essence, they barely knew him, and yet everyone at the farm had opened their family to him.

The generosity was overwhelming, and Lachlan hoped he could live up to that.

Abe slid across the bench seat, wrapping his arm around Lachlan, and he scooted closer. Lachlan turned and kissed Abe, leaning closer to deepen the kiss. "I didn't bring you up here for anything other than to watch the view."

Lachlan pulled back, skin stinging as though he'd been slapped. "Oh." He turned, looking out the side window as his cheeks heated with intense embarrassment.

"Okay, that didn't sound right. I don't want to do anything here. Grandma Katie and Harriet are going to the movies this evening, and Foster made a big deal of saying that he and Javi were going out as well." Abe's eyes glinted in the reflected sunlight when Lachlan turned back to face him. "So I thought we could make love properly."

Lachlan wasn't sure how he felt about doing anything in the farmhouse. He was a guest of sorts, and that seemed out of bounds to him. Abe, however, seemed to think nothing of it, and when he licked and sucked at the base of Lachlan's neck, he groaned softly and leaned into the heated action. "But…."

"Do you think the others arranged to go out on the same night by accident?" Abe chuckled and tugged him closer. "This is only the warm-up act for what's to come later."

Lachlan quivered when Abe slid a hand under his shirt and up his chest, tweaking a nipple before rubbing tiny circles in an ever-increasing array of intense sensations, capped off by Abe's lips touching his with the slight electric thrill of passion. He was on fire, his cock aching in his pants. Lachlan silently willed Abe to move his hand lower and help him out, but he showed no signs of it. Lachlan clamped his eyes closed as desire built more and more until he figured he wasn't going to be able to contain it. Then Abe stopped, tugging his hand away, leaving Lachlan breathless and wondering what the hell was going on. "Abe…." God, he sounded almost mournfully plaintive, even to himself.

Abe chuckled. "I know exactly how you feel." He slid back behind the wheel and started the engine. "We should head back to the farm before I forget myself and all the things I have planned for this evening." He sat still, breathing the same way Lachlan was, and once Lachlan strapped himself in, Abe slowly drove them down the hill.

ABE DROPPED him at the farm, saying he needed to go home to get a few things done for his brother, but that he'd be back that evening. Lachlan went inside and found Harriet and Grandma Katie at the kitchen table with a few of the ladies from church, talking over coffee.

"Did you have a good time with Abe?" Harriet asked.

Lachlan fingered the medallion at his throat without thinking and smiled. "Yes." He kissed both Harriet and Grandma Katie on the cheek. "The party was such a huge surprise and I appreciate it so much… along with everything else."

"We were happy to do it," Harriet said, squeezing his hand.

"Is there anything you need me to do tonight?"

Grandma Katie shook her head. "The four of us are going to dinner and then a movie. I understand Abe will be back, so the two of you should have the house to yourselves." The wicked glint in her eye told him all he needed to know about just what she expected to happen while they were gone. "There are plenty of leftovers in the refrigerator, so help yourselves to whatever you want." She patted his hand.

"Thanks." He squeezed her hand back and left the ladies to talk, heading for the stairs.

"I knew his mother and thought the world of her," one of the church ladies said. Lachlan wasn't sure who she was, but it didn't matter. That his mother was well thought of and liked was all that was important.

Up in his room, he closed the door and sat on the edge of the bed, looking at the photograph of his mother that rested on the stand. "I'm doing everything I can. But, dang it, I miss you so much." He sighed. "I'll come visit you just as soon as I can. I promise. But Harriet and Grandma Katie had a nice party for me, and I got some nice things." Of course, he'd have traded it all in a heartbeat to have her back. But those were wishes that would never come true, and there was no use hanging his heart on them.

CHAPTER 10

AT HOME, Abe changed clothes and hurried out to the equipment shed to check on the tractor and make a few adjustments to ensure the old girl was running as well as could be expected.

"Do you and Lachlan have plans for tonight?" Randy asked as Abe was finishing up.

"Yeah. Nothing too huge or anything." That was a lie, but Randy didn't need to know the details of what he and Lachlan would be doing. "You're good to go on the tractor. Just baby it along and we'll make it through the season." Thank goodness that, for the most part, tractors like the one they had were relatively simple and could still be worked on at the farm. The newer ones had a lot of modern gadgets and required specialized equipment to care for them. "What else did you need me to do?"

"Nothing, I guess." Randy looked toward the house. "I think you and Dad really need to talk."

Abe sighed. He didn't think another talk with his dad was going to yield anything. "I have to go in and change again. I'll pop my head in." That was the most he could agree to. "Are you on to milk the herd?"

"I just finished, and Dad just went inside." Randy tossed him one more serious look and left.

Abe closed up the shed before heading inside. He found his dad in the living room, sitting in his favorite chair, already half-asleep. "Hey."

His dad started slightly and reached to the table next to him. "I understand your young man graduated today." He sounded uncomfortable. "It's all over town what he and those girls did."

"Yes, Dad."

His dad lifted a white card envelope. "Have they found the reverend's kid yet?"

"Not as far as I know."

His dad handed the card to him, and Abe read Lachlan's name on it. "Randy said you were going out tonight, and I was hoping you could take this to your friend. He did a brave thing. I can see that now." He sat up straighter in his chair.

"Lachlan is brave and a lot more." Abe came closer to his dad. "He lost his mom, the way Randy and I did, and he's doing his best to try to move on. It's hard, but he's doing what he can. He's going to college in the fall, and he's staying with Foster and Harriet until then."

"So he's leaving eventually," his father observed. "They all leave."

Jesus. He and his father shared the same fear. That was a new one. "That's not necessarily true. Mom didn't leave us—she was taken. And you need to move on from that." He figured he may as well go for broke. "Allow yourself to be happy again, Dad. Mom would want things that way."

"Don't you think I've tried?"

Abe shrugged. "No. I think you stayed in a bubble and tried to do everything the way you always have and never changed a thing around here because you're afraid that you'd lose some of Mom if you did." Everything in the house was as close to how their mom left it as possible. His dad's bedroom was nearly exactly as it had been then. "If the farm is going to be viable, we all need to move on, and that means you have to stop sitting in the chair and get out there and help Randy make the changes you both need to. This farm is more than a one-person job."

"Yeah, and I asked you to come help."

"Dad, the second person that this farm needs is you." Abe stood over his father and glared at him. "Randy has some great ideas and he's trying to make a difference, but the two of you need to do it together. Build the herd back up to full strength. Add some different products that you can take to market. Make the most of the land and the resources you have. As much as you want me to step in, I can't. I really think this needs to be something that you and Randy do together. He's the future of this farm, not me."

Just like that, a vision for his future clicked into place and he wasn't here on the farm. He knew what he wanted… or at least what he hoped to try, and that meant he wasn't going to be tied to milking cows twice a day for the rest of his life.

"You sure seem to have all the answers all of a sudden," his dad groused, but leaned forward and lifted himself out of the chair. "And you're probably right. I know this farm better than anyone."

"Yes, you do. So make it work again."

His father nodded, and instead of sinking back into his chair, he went out through the kitchen. He grunted the way he always did as he pulled on his boots. "Be sure to give your friend his card."

"I will." Abe hurried up the stairs, where he showered and changed clothes, then ran back down and out to his truck. He waved to his dad and Randy as they talked in the yard, and pulled away, happy and hopeful that his dad would make the changes needed to return the farm to the success it had always been.

Abe was no longer a part of that world; at least, he didn't see himself that way any longer. The farm was Randy's and his dad's futures. His lay elsewhere, and Abe couldn't help thinking that his chances and opportunities might lie in a completely different direction.

He pulled into the otherwise empty farmyard as the sun was getting ready to set, filling the sky with reds and golds, wisps of clouds intensifying the color. It was a gorgeous evening, with the promise of summer and everything it would bring hanging in the warmth of a late-spring evening. The cows lowed in the nearby fields as they munched their evening meals, calling to one another, their voices floating on the wind. Abe stood listening for a few seconds and then went inside through the back door.

"Lachlan," Abe called, then listened for a response. He didn't receive one, which he thought was strange. Hell, with everyone gone and how excited Lachlan had been earlier, Abe half expected to be jumped upon entry.

A scrape deeper in the house reached his ears, and Abe moved through the kitchen to the living room and then the front room. "Are you upstairs?" The little minx.

He took the steps two at a time and hurried down to Lachlan's room, which was empty. That was strange. Concerned, Abe listened once more. The scraping came again, only fainter, and Abe might have questioned whether he'd actually heard it at all if he hadn't been so intent on finding Lachlan. He returned to the stairs and took them quickly, wondering where in the heck Lachlan could be. Something was most definitely wrong.

The crash of broken glass led him to the pantry off the kitchen. He yanked open the door. Eddie stood with his back to him, dripping in red, and for a second, Abe thought it might have been blood, but it was too purple. The scent of grape reached his nose.

Abe went icy when the light from the kitchen glinted off the cold steel of the gun in Eddie's hand. No matter how silly the scene appeared at first glance, reality thrummed in quickly. Eddie was seriously deadly and had his sights on Lachlan, who stood pressed to the back wall of the large pantry. Abe tried to keep his cool, but it was hard as hell when every ounce of his being screamed to throw himself between them and protect Lachlan, the man who held his heart. The thought of losing him permanently set his knees quaking.

"So help me God, I'll blow your brains out, both of you, if you try anything like that again." Eddie waved a pistol in Abe's direction, then pointed it back at Lachlan. "If you want your little boyfriend to stay in one piece, then sit on the floor and don't fucking move." As Abe slid to the floor, Eddie wiped grape juice off his face, reached for Lachlan, and slammed him against the back wall. "Pull that shit again and I'll do a hell of a lot worse than beat the shit out of you." The gun wavered, and Abe wondered what in the hell Eddie was thinking by coming here. What exactly did he expect to get from Lachlan?

"Yeah. Bully me like you did everyone else. You're sick, Eddie, and you know it." Lachlan ducked a punch and reached for another jar of Grandma Katie's homemade grape juice.

Eddie grabbed his arm and tossed him against the wall again. Abe got to his feet, but Eddie turned the gun on him. "I don't care which of you two I shoot. My life is over anyway. My dad won't have anything to do with me because of you and your fucking big mouths. Who cares about a few girls and shit they can't remember anyway? They deserved what they got, leading guys on all the time and then not delivering. I was just making sure I got what I paid for." Spittle flew from Eddie's lips as he ranted on, and Abe watched Lachlan closely, trying to tell him to calm down. That was the only way to pull Eddie back from the edge of hysteria.

Lachlan didn't seem to be getting the message at all. "Paid for? You can't buy people. What kind of sick piece of shit are you?" he asked, even as he caught Abe's gaze. Lachlan tilted his head slightly to the side, where a single jar of vegetables sat alone on a shelf. Now Abe understood what was going on and nodded very slightly.

Eddie spun back toward Lachlan. "Shut the hell up! I bought them dinner… a nice dinner, and they needed to put out. Instead they all asked to be taken home or some such crap." Eddie's breathing came rapidly, and Abe wondered if he'd been using some of the things in his pharmacopoeia himself. "All I did was give them something that lowered their inhibitions so they'd do what they really wanted to do. The stuff is harmless, and afterward they were all begging for it."

"No, they weren't," Lachlan countered, and Eddie slapped him, the crack echoing in the small space. Lachlan raised a hand to his face, covering the red spot. "Go ahead and hit me, but that isn't going to change the fact that you're a rapist. You hurt people and used them."

Eddie shook with fury as he moved in on Lachlan again. This time Abe reached for a large can and brought it down full strength toward Eddie's head. At the last second, Eddie moved, and the can smashed into his shoulder. Bone cracked, and Eddie let out a roar that filled the small space. Somehow he held on to the gun and swung around toward Abe. Lachlan pounced, pushing Eddie into the built-in wooden shelving, one of which collapsed and sent a rain of canned

162

goods pelting down on him. He roared again before being hit in the head and slumping to the floor.

Abe got the gun away from Eddie and out of the room before he came to, groaning and swearing up a storm.

"That's enough," Lachlan said. "Abe, call the police and tell them we have the fugitive they've been looking for."

Abe nodded and nearly laughed. Eddie was covered in grape juice, bits of vegetables, some blood, and surrounded by cans of soup and beans. He made the call, and when Eddie tried to get up, Lachlan kicked his feet out from under him. Abe got through and explained where they were and what had happened. He hung up when the operator said they'd send someone right out. Abe glared at Eddie. "Try getting up again and I'll bash your head with soup cans." He'd had more than enough of this asshole to last him a lifetime.

It took ten minutes for the police to arrive. Lachlan let them in, showed them the gun, and then led them to the pantry, where the two men in uniform gaped at a whimpering Eddie marinating in grape juice.

Lachlan explained what had happened. "I had taken a shower and came down to see what I needed to do for dinner. I found Eddie in the kitchen, and he forced me into the pantry. He wanted to make me pay for turning him in and helping the ladies he'd hurt. Apparently Eddie feels that he has the right to act any way he wants. I have no doubt he intended to hurt me, but Abe returned, and Eddie closed the pantry door and told me if I moved or made noise, he'd shoot me."

"What's with the grape juice?"

"I beaned him with one of Grandma Katie's quarts of it. Shame to waste it, but I'd hoped to knock him out." Lachlan sighed and stayed away as the officers cuffed Eddie and took possession of the handgun he'd been using.

The officers asked a lot of questions and seemed satisfied with their answers. They took pictures of the mess and the area before getting ready to leave.

"Can I clean up the mess? You know Harriet and Grandma Katie will have a fit if they find their pantry like this."

"It's fine. We have what we need," the officer in charge told them.

Once they left, Lachlan went into near-manic mode, putting everything back the way it was like some sort of cleaning whirlwind.

"You know they'll understand."

"Yes, they will. But if we can get things back to normal, Harriet and Grandma Katie aren't going to feel as violated by the intrusion than if they come home to a huge mess." Lachlan's hands and arms moved at a mile a minute, wiping down shelves and restacking the cans.

Abe cleaned up the glass and wiped down the floors. It was pretty obvious that something had indeed happened, considering the broken shelving and the old linoleum that now had a slight purple tinge that wasn't going to come out no matter how hard Abe scrubbed.

"It's all right," Abe said after a while, gently taking Lachlan into his arms, stilling his frenetic movements and just holding him. "Both of us are safe." He took the can from Lachlan's hand and set it on the shelf. "You need to settle down and breathe." He spun Lachlan around, wrapped him in his arms, and waited for the tension to leave his body.

They stood together for a long while, Lachlan rigid, even shaking, and then, slowly, first the shaking and then the rigidity subsided and Lachlan's arm extended around his neck. Finally Lachlan slumped against him. "Today was so nice, and then that bastard had to do this."

"He isn't going to be able to hurt anyone anymore." God, Abe certainly hoped that was true. He held Lachlan tighter and let him shake against him. Abe was really beginning to understand that what Lachlan needed was stability and routine, and he probably would for quite a while. And as the bigger picture of what those needs might look like began to come together in his head, it meshed neatly with the images of how he saw his own future. Up until now he truly hadn't seen a way forward for them, but it was possible, and it was up to Abe to try to make it happen.

"Everything good seems to turn to crap somehow." Lachlan wiped his eyes. "Instead of today being my high school graduation, I'm going to remember it as the day I was held at gunpoint."

"It's still your high school graduation, and don't forget that when you remember the whole held at gunpoint thing, you stood up to him and beaned the guy with a grape juice grenade." Abe smiled, and Lachlan stopped shaking. "He looked like Violet from Willy Wonka. He was purple everywhere." He paused, and Lachlan snickered, which was the exact reaction Abe was hoping for.

"Then you hit him with the mixed vegetables and he looked like a bizarre salad." Lachlan laughed a little harder. "And to top it off, he got beaned with a can of beans." He smiled full-on and some of the tension dissipated.

"Did Eddie ever say what he wanted? Why would he come here and not get away while he had the chance?"

Lachlan's smile faded. "Typical bully. He could never let someone else get anything over on him. All he kept talking about was that he was a laughingstock and it was all my fault. I didn't hurt those girls and I didn't tell him to do it. His actions were his responsibility." Lachlan took a deep breath. "At least he's gone, but he sure did screw up date night."

Abe sighed. All the time he'd hoped the two of them would have alone had pretty much been thrown out the window. Not that it really mattered. He took Lachlan's hand and led him to the living room, where he turned on the television and found an Indiana Jones movie. There would be action, spills, ridiculous plot holes, and plenty to make fun of as they watched. And this was the one with Indiana's father. Even better. "Just sit and relax."

The sun was setting outside and the light through the windows darkened as they settled together on the sofa. It was mindless fun, and as the room grew darker, they ended up closer and closer until Lachlan rested his head on Abe's shoulder. As Indiana and his father raced away into the sunset at the end of the film, Abe realized Lachlan was asleep, breathing gently into his ear. Abe turned off the television, and Lachlan lifted his head.

The room was dark, with only the light from the outside floods filtering inside, casting soft shadows when they heard a car pull into the drive. Lachlan tensed, and Abe did his best to calm him as Harriet and Grandma Katie came in the back door. Both of them stopped inside, and Abe met them at the kitchen table to explain about earlier.

"I hope you kicked his ass," Grandma Katie said, hands on her hips. "Waste of perfectly good grape juice if you ask me, but I'm glad Lachlan got a good hit in."

"Eddie's in custody now, and you'll need to go in and file breaking-and-entering charges in the morning. Apparently they want as much as they can get so they can be sure to hold him," Abe said.

"I don't think Eddie's all there anymore," Lachlan explained softly. "He was talking crazy and not making a whole lot of sense. I hope they get him the help he needs." He sank into one of the chairs, and Grandma Katie checked out the pantry, remarking that the mess had been well cleaned up, and then started in making sandwiches.

"Are you really okay, sweetheart?" she asked Lachlan as she put a plate in front of him.

"I guess so. He came after me, and I threw the first thing I had at hand at him. I knew that he wasn't going to get me to go anywhere with him and that Abe was in the house. Even with Eddie holding me and his hand over my mouth, I knew I needed to make some noise. So I bit him hard and threw the jar at him. He was still dripping when the police took him away."

"And when the cans fell off the shelf, he got beaned on the head with one of the cans of beans," Abe interjected.

"What could that boy have been thinking?" Harriet asked.

"He wasn't, that's all there is to it." Grandma Katie put more sandwiches on the table and admonished them all to eat. "It sure doesn't look like any of us is getting much sleep tonight." She took a chair herself, and they all ate and talked quietly until Foster and Javi got home. At that point, the stories were shared all over again, and Foster picked up the phone to make some calls. Even at close to midnight, he was able to get some answers.

"He's in custody and that's where he's staying. I said we'd be pressing charges as well, and they have enough to hold him for a long time. So we can all go on to bed, and I'll make sure everything is locked up tight."

No one said a word when Abe took Lachlan upstairs and they disappeared into Lachlan's room together.

CHAPTER 11

LACHLAN GOT ready for bed but was only going through the motions. It wasn't until Abe got in bed with him, holding him tight, warmth pressed right to him from legs to back, that Lachlan was able to relax. His mother had always said that sometimes one thing built on another, and he sure hoped everything was done with its building, because if there was more crap to be piled on, he wasn't going to be able to handle any of it.

"Just relax and try not to think about it."

"But I keep wondering if he'll get out and come back," Lachlan said, his voice sounding small even to him.

"It's over. He's in custody and facing so many charges that it's going to take an hour to read them all in court."

"But I was so scared." He'd nearly wet himself when Eddie had first grabbed him. Not something to be proud of, and he fully intended to keep that to himself.

"Maybe," Abe said, rubbing Lachlan's belly. "But I think you were brave as hell. You defended yourself, and once you thought you had the upper hand, you didn't back down and made Eddie do stupid things. He kept looking at you, and that allowed me to get a whack at him." Abe barely whispered into the darkness, but it sounded so loud to Lachlan. "You were cool and collected, and even when he hit you, you stood your ground, and that had to unnerve him. Bullies only understand fear, and when you didn't show any, he wasn't sure what to do."

"I didn't do that much."

Abe propped himself up on his elbow and gently rolled Lachlan onto his back. "You were amazing. Bravery is doing what you need to, regardless of how scared you are. Everyone gets scared—you'd be crazy not to. But you were still able to think and keep Eddie guessing. That took real courage and fortitude. So don't forget that." Abe leaned down to kiss him, and Lachlan pulled Abe down on top of him. He wanted to forget all about it and just feel for a while.

"Make it all stop," Lachlan whispered, and Abe seemed to know exactly what he needed.

Abe's weight pressed to him, his lips possessing Lachlan's. He held on and let Abe take charge and was so amazed he did. Abe played him like a violin for longer than Lachlan thought possible, using his hands and mouth to drive Lachlan to the heights of passion, pull back, and do it again over and over until Lachlan had very little concept of time or of anything outside the bedroom. All that mattered was the head-to-toe tingling, breathless anticipation, and Abe's taste on his lips. When Abe entered him, slowly, Lachlan was as keyed up as he'd ever been in his life, and the sensation, still new and exciting, pushed him over the edge within a matter of minutes. He was too overwhelmed to cry out or even groan. All he could manage to do was hold on to Abe and let the wave of ecstasy take him wherever it wanted to go. By the time he closed his eyes to breathe through the afterglow, he'd truly forgotten his name, let alone the rest of the evening's goings-on.

That didn't mean he was able to fall asleep. The crap with Eddie had faded somewhat from his immediate thoughts, but others wound their way in.

"Abe," he said softly.

"Yeah." Abe sounded asleep, and Lachlan wished he'd kept quiet.

"Sorry. Just go back to sleep." He stilled, hoping Abe would just do as he asked.

"What is it?" Abe scooted closer, his leg sliding along Lachlan's. "I'm awake." He moaned and kissed Lachlan's shoulder.

"I'm not sure what's going to happen. I mean, I know it's the end of May and I don't go to school until late August, but what are we going to do?"

"Well... I have some money that my mother left me, as well as some savings from working here. So I was thinking I'd get a job and

169

go with you to Lansing. There are plenty of places I can work, and I thought that you and I could get a place to live together."

Lachlan smiled and rolled over. "That's a very sweet thought, but no. I don't want you doing that."

Abe gasped. "You don't want me with you?"

"Of course I do. But what kind of job are you going to get? A barista at Starbucks or making paninis at Panera? Is that what you want to do for four years while I study? You'll hate me because you'll be bored and alone a lot of the time. The people you care about are here, and I can't take you away from them." Lachlan looked in Abe's eyes. "Before my mom died, I was this stupid kid who thought that everything was ahead of him and that I had my life pretty mapped out. Then everything fell apart and I was alone. I lost my mom, but I also lost my home. That's what I really want."

"I don't understand."

Lachlan took Abe's hand and interlaced their fingers. "I want a home, something that no one can take away from me. I want a place to come back to that's mine and that I know is there and will always be there. That home isn't going to be some dingy apartment in Lansing that we rent because I'm a student and you're working at Panera. I want a real home. So I'm going to go to school so I can have the skills to help us make that come true."

"Okay?" Abe clearly didn't get what Lachlan was driving at, and maybe he wasn't being clear, but Lachlan soldiered on.

"Start laying the groundwork. Harriet, Grandma Katie, Foster, and Javi are as close to a family… a home… as I have right now. But that can be taken away. You are the one I want to build my own home with."

"So… what do you want me to do?" Abe asked cautiously. He still wasn't getting the picture.

"Well, I've been thinking. I want to be an engineer, and I'm thinking that process engineering for things like dairy products might be a good place to start. I was thinking that maybe you and I could have a farm of our own, maybe with cows, or maybe something else. But it would be ours. Land and a place to call our own. And if you want to use the money your mother left you for something, then that will make a good down payment if you want."

"What do we do about things in the meantime?" He bit his lower lip nervously.

"That's easy. I go to school, and you either come visit me or come get me every few weeks. We spend holidays and vacations together and use that time to figure out what we want to do."

"It sounds like you have things all mapped out."

"Nope. It's just my idea of things. But just like you told me that I needed to go to school to make the most of myself, I'm not going to let you follow me so you can do anything less. Your life is here, and you understand everything that goes on here. You know all about raising cattle and the products made from them. You've helped Foster build this farm into a successful business. So together we work toward a place of our own that we can do that exact same thing with. My going to school is a part of that, and you staying here and keeping your eyes open is your part."

"Because there will be an opportunity that we can take advantage of."

"Probably. I want to think that this farm is my home, and I don't want to lose it. The people here are kind and caring. They'll take good care of you when I can't be here."

"But who will take care of you?" Abe asked.

"That will be your job when I come home to visit." Lachlan leaned closer. "I may be away at school, but it will always be you that I'm coming home to. This place... this town... you. I know this is Foster and Harriet's farm, but I can't think of this place without thinking of you. So it's like you're my home, and I need you here so I always know right where it is." Lachlan wiped his eyes. It was late and he hoped he was making sense.

"But what if you're away at school and you meet some dashing, handsome young man who makes your heart go pitter-pat, and you decide that I'm too boring and stink of cow crap all the time? And this guy smells of expensive cologne and drives a really nice car, and—"

Lachlan rolled his eyes. "And his name will be Prince Charming and he'll be followed right behind by some chick in a huge blue dress with glass slippers. I may be young, but I know my own heart. See, my life was in ruins, and you helped me put body, mind, and soul back together again. That isn't something that you forget. It's what you carry with you, deep down, for the rest of your life." There was no doubt about that for Lachlan.

He slid closer to Abe and snuggled in. The future road ahead was sure to contain many twists and turns, but some things Lachlan knew he could count on, and the man lying next to him, holding him as though he was the most precious person in the world, was definitely one of those.

EPILOGUE

LACHLAN GRABBED the last box and raced down the dorm stairs and out to the parking lot where Abe had met him every few weeks for the last two years. He waved to some of his friends as he passed to reach Abe's truck. He put the box in the back along with the rest of his things, not that there was much. When Abe had come to pick him up a few weeks ago, Lachlan had already packed what he didn't think he was going to need, so all he had were his final things anyway.

"Are you ready to go?" Abe asked.

"Yes, but we need to make a stop on our way home. I found an extruder for Foster." Lachlan climbed into the truck, bouncing on the seat, he was so excited. "Pierre's dad bought it at an auction a few years ago. He had the bright idea to make his own ice cream. It never got off the ground, but he had the scaled extruder and he's willing to sell it. So we need to take a look, and if it passes muster, Foster said to bring it home."

The creamery had been Foster's idea, but Javi had run with it in an amazing way, and their ice cream and increased artisan cheese production were a huge success. They ended up buying all of Randy's eggs, and he was adding more chickens to supply what they needed. The success of the creamery had an amazing ripple effect. What surprised them all was how quickly Javi became associated with the products, so now they had Javi's brand of ice cream and cheese, which had just been picked up by Meijer's and was being distributed across the state in the luxury foods section. The problem was that packaging was still done by hand and they needed to make the process faster, hence the extruder that they could use to fill and weigh the containers.

"Then let's go. Everyone is excited to see you. Grace wanted to come as well." A few months ago, a stray black lab, scrawny and undernourished, had wandered onto the farm and adopted all of them. With her huge brown eyes, how could any of them have turned her away?

"Of course. You know I'm her favorite," Lachlan said with a grin. Grace loved him.

"That's because you sneak her treats every chance you get." Abe pulled out of the parking lot and wound through campus to the main road leading to the freeway. "So, two down and two to go."

"That's right, though if things work out and the classes are offered when I need them, I should be able to graduate a semester early. That would be awesome." He was tired of school at the moment and ready to spend some time with the family. "I have some ideas to share with Foster and Javi about the creamery."

"When haven't you?" Abe said gently. Each semester Lachlan had returned with some things they could do to improve their processes, and Foster had implemented quite a few of them.

"Three whole months," Lachlan said softly. He had three months to spend with Abe and Grace, Harriet and Grandma Katie, Foster and Javi…. To be at home.

"It's going to be busy because I think I might have found a farm for us. The Morgans, up the road a few miles from Foster and Javi, are looking to retire. Some of the other farms have been interested in buying them out, but they don't want to see what they've worked for all their lives just gobbled up and becoming part of one of the other farms. The cool part is that there's a small orchard that Mrs. Morgan planted a few years ago. She wanted some fruit trees, so Mr. Morgan planted them for her. Unfortunately, after that she broke her knees and hadn't been able to do a whole lot with it. But the trees just need some pruning, and we could get them into shape quickly and they'd start producing right away. Foster is looking for additional reliable sources of milk for the creamery, and the Morgans have a great herd. So, we could buy that along with the land and the farmhouse. I haven't talked price with them yet, but I think we can reach a good deal. You know

174

the farm—we helped out there last summer when Mr. Morgan had to take his wife into the hospital for a few days."

"Is that the place? It's really nice, and the barn was in good shape." He remembered looking over the milking equipment and thinking how new it all was.

"It is, and Mr. Morgan is real fussy about pretty much everything. He said we can look it over when you get home and decide. He hasn't told many people yet because he doesn't want the buzzards to start circling."

Lachlan nodded. "So how would all this work?"

"Well, I think we need to talk to Foster. His idea was that we'd buy the Morgan farm and you and I would live there. We'd combine operations with Foster, and we would buy into the bigger operation. So instead of owning our own farm with all the risks that entails, we'd own part of the larger enterprise with Harriet, Foster, and Javi. Foster thought we could expand the orchard on part of the property to add to the produce we take to market and for use in the products in the creamery. It would also give us a larger source of milk for ice cream and cheese."

"But what do the Morgans think?" Abe had just said that they didn't want to combine their farms.

"That's the beauty of it. They trust Foster, so they're in agreement. We all just need to look everything over and decide if it's what we want to do." Abe was clearly excited as all get-out, and Lachlan caught some of it.

"Okay. Then let's look at it." The thought of a home of their own was almost too good to be true. It was happening quicker than Lachlan thought it would, but he'd learned to go with the opportunities.

Abe reached across the seat, and Lachlan took his hand, holding it tightly. This was what he missed when he was away at school, the ability to touch Abe whenever he wanted to.

They drove for nearly an hour, then got off the freeway, following the directions Lachlan had to a ranch house on a large lot. They stopped and got out. His friend Pierre met them and showed them the machine.

"Mom wants it out of the garage," Pierre said as Lachlan looked it over. It shone with glittering stainless steel, and its clean, compact frame looked really good. He plugged it in and checked it over before paying what Pierre's dad wanted. It was worth every penny.

Lachlan disassembled it as much as he could, removing the legs and hopper attachments. Then they loaded it and the pieces into the truck after wrapping it in a fresh tarp, and an hour later, they were on their way.

"Do you really think it will work?" Abe asked.

"Yes. I'm going to have to make a few modifications, but I think we can fix it so the freezers discharge right into the hopper, so we can freeze, weigh, and package in a single step. That should save a lot of time."

They stopped for a snack along the way, and Lachlan took the opportunity to share a kiss—or three—with Abe while they waited in the drive-through line. They ate as they rode, with Lachlan getting more and more excited the closer they got.

By the time Abe pulled into the farm drive, Lachlan could barely contain himself. Grace bounded out to meet them, and Lachlan raced out of the truck to pet her coat as she wriggled around him, whining because he wasn't petting her fast enough. Harriet came out of the house to hug him, along with Grandma Katie, who now used a cane to help with her balance, though it didn't slow her down any.

"You got it," Foster said, greeting both of them and turning his attention to the machine.

"Yup. We'll install it as soon as I can clean it thoroughly. Maybe next week," Lachlan said, just as excited as Foster and Javi.

"And he's already got ideas on how to integrate it with the freezers."

"Of course he does," Javi said, hugging him. "That's our engineer."

They got the truck unloaded and the new equipment stowed away. Lachlan had plenty of help bringing in his things. It was like their long-lost son had come home, and Lachlan realized that maybe he had. This house, these people, felt like home to him.

"Dinner is in an hour," Harriet said.

"Good. Then I'm going to steal him for a while," Abe said, ushering Lachlan back out to the truck.

The drive was familiar, like everything else had been. But this was special. He didn't need Abe to say a word about where he was taking him. The hill was the same, and the view from the top just like it had been the first time Abe had brought him up there. As they stopped in their usual spot and Lachlan got out and sat on the lowered tailgate, he looked out over the valley.

Abe sat next to him, his arm sliding around Lachlan's waist, and he leaned against him, natural as anything in the world. The farm, the people in his life who loved him, and the man sitting right next to him—they were familiar and welcoming, as unchanging in the big picture as he could have asked for. No one was going to take this life away from him, because it was what they all wanted. Abe leaned closer and kissed him gently at first, but the need and desire from weeks of separation took over for a few minutes.

"We have all the time in the world," Abe said, even as Lachlan's heart hammered in his ears.

He nodded, and they sat so close together, Lachlan would've had to have been on Abe's lap to be any nearer. He was home—his permanent, forever, no one was going to take it away home. Just what he'd said he'd wanted. Lachlan turned, sliding his hand around Abe's neck, and guided their lips together, kissing his dream come true.

ANDREW GREY grew up in western Michigan with a father who loved to tell stories and a mother who loved to read them. Since then he has lived all over the country and traveled throughout the world. He has a master's degree from the University of Wisconsin-Milwaukee and now works full-time on his writing. Andrew's hobbies include collecting antiques, gardening, and leaving his dirty dishes anywhere but in the sink (particularly when writing). He considers himself blessed with an accepting family, fantastic friends, and the world's most supportive and loving husband. Andrew currently lives in beautiful historic Carlisle, Pennsylvania.

E-mail: andrewgrey@comcast.net
Website: www.andrewgreybooks.com

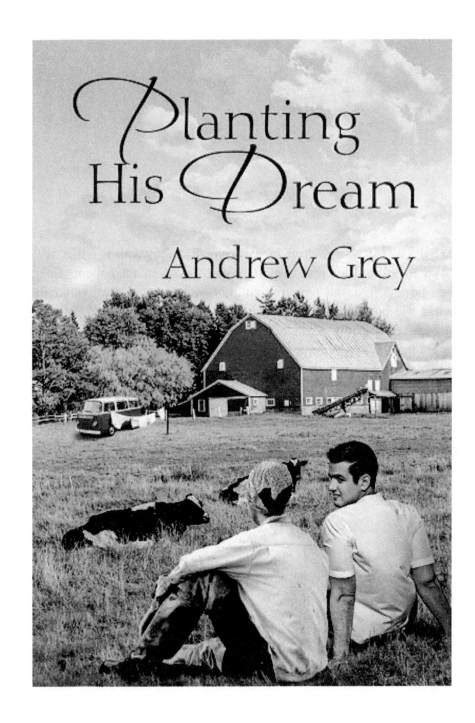

Planting His Dream

Andrew Grey

Planting Dreams: Book One

Foster dreams of getting away, but after his father's death, he has to take over the family dairy farm. It soon becomes clear his father hasn't been doing the best job of running it, so not only does Foster need to take over the day-to-day operations, he also needs to find new ways of bringing in revenue.

Javi has no time to dream. He and his family are migrant workers, and daily survival is a struggle, so they travel to anywhere they can get work. When they arrive in their old van, Foster arranges for Javi to help him on the farm.

To Javi's surprise, Foster listens to his ideas and actually puts them into action. Over days that turn into weeks, they grow to like and then care for each other, but they come from two very different worlds, and they both have responsibilities to their families that neither can walk away from. Is it possible for them to discover a dream they can share? Perhaps they can plant their own and nurture it together to see it grow, if their different backgrounds don't separate them forever.

www.dreamspinnerpress.com

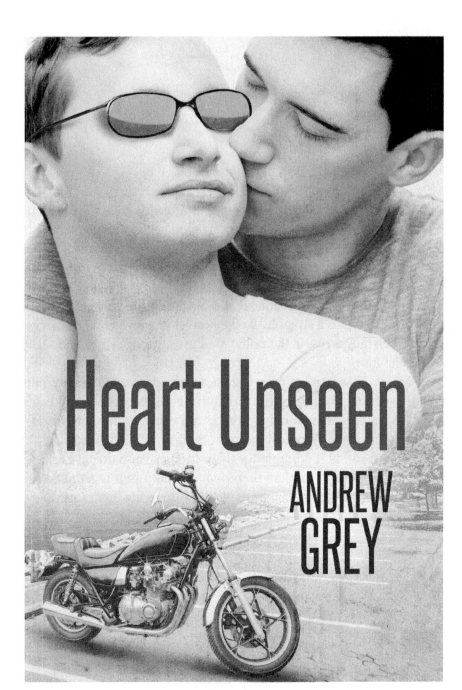

Heart Unseen

ANDREW GREY

As a stunningly attractive man and the owner of a successful chain of auto repair garages, Trevor is used to attention, adoration, and getting what he wants. What he wants tends to be passionate, no-strings-attached flings with men he meets in clubs. He doesn't expect anything different when he sets his sights on James. Imagine his surprise when the charm that normally brings men to their knees fails to impress. Trevor will need to drop the routine and connect with James on a meaningful level. He starts by offering to take James home instead of James riding home with his intoxicated friend.

For James, losing his sight at a young age meant limited opportunities for social interaction. Spending most of his time working at a school for the blind has left him unfamiliar with Trevor's world, but James has fought hard for his independence, and he knows what he wants. Right now, that means stepping outside his comfort zone and into Trevor's heart.

Trevor is also open to exploring real love and commitment for a change, but before he can be the man James needs him to be, he'll have to deal with the pain of his past.

www.dreamspinnerpress.com

DREAMSPUN
DESIRES

POPPY'S SECRET

Andrew Grey

A second chance born
of love.

A second chance born of love.

Pat Corrigan and Edgerton "Edge" Winters were ready to start a family—or so Pat thought. At the last minute, Edge got cold feet and fled. Pat didn't bother telling him the conception had already gone through and little Emma was on her way. He didn't want a relationship based on obligation. He'd rather raise his daughter on his own.

Nine years later, Emma and her Poppy are doing fine. Edge isn't. He realizes what he threw away by leaving, and he's back to turn his life around and reclaim his family. It'll take a lot to prove to Pat that he's a new man, and even if Edge succeeds, the secret Pat has hidden for years might shatter their dreams all over again.

www.dreamspinnerpress.com

REKINDLED FLAME

ANDREW GREY

Rekindled Flame: Book One

Firefighter Morgan has worked hard to build a home for himself after a nomadic childhood. When Morgan is called to a fire, he finds the family out front, but their tenant still inside. He rescues Richard Smalley, who turns out to be an old friend he hasn't seen in years and the one person he regretted leaving behind.

Richard has had a hard life. He served in the military, where he lost the use of his legs, and has been struggling to make his way since coming home. Now that he no longer has a place to live, Morgan takes him in, but when someone attempts to set fire to Morgan's house, they both become suspicious and wonder what's going on.

Years ago Morgan was gutted when he moved away, leaving Richard behind, so he's happy to pick things up where they left off. But now that Richard seems to be the target of an arsonist, he may not be the safest person to be around.

www.dreamspinnerpress.com

SETTING
the HOOK
ANDREW GREY

It could be the catch of a lifetime.

William Westmoreland escapes his unfulfilling Rhode Island existence by traveling to Florida twice a year and chartering Mike Jansen's fishing boat to take him out on the Gulf. The crystal-blue water and tropical scenery isn't the only view William enjoys, but he's never made his move. A vacation romance just isn't on his horizon.

Mike started his Apalachicola charter fishing service as a way to care for his daughter and mother, putting their safety and security ahead of the needs of his own heart. Denying his attraction becomes harder with each of William's visits.

William and Mike's latest fishing excursion starts with a beautiful day, but a hurricane's erratic course changes everything, stranding William. As the wind and rain rage outside, the passion the two men have been trying to resist for years crashes over them. In the storm's wake, it leaves both men yearning to prolong what they have found. But real life pulls William back to his obligations. Can they find a way to reduce the distance between them and discover a place where their souls can meet? The journey will require rough sailing, but the bright future at the end might be worth the choppy seas.

www.dreamspinnerpress.com